PATRICK GALE

The Whole Day Through

FOURTH ESTATE • *London*

Fourth Estate
An imprint of HarperCollins*Publishers*
77–85 Fulham Palace Road, Hammersmith, London W6 8JB

www.4thestate.co.uk
Visit our authors' blog at www.fifthestate.co.uk
Love this book? www.bookarmy.com

This Fourth Estate edition published 2009
1

First published by Fourth Estate in 2009

A catalogue record for this book is available from the British Library

ISBN 978-0-00-730601-5

Set in Sabon by G&M Designs Limited, Raunds, Northamptonshire

Printed and bound in Great Britain by Clays Ltd, St Ives plc

Mixed Sources

Product group from well-managed
forests and other controlled sources
www.fsc.org Cert no. SW-COC-1806
© 1996 Forest Stewardship Council

FSC

FSC is a non-profit international organisation established to promote the
responsible management of the world's forests. Products carrying the FSC
label are independently certified to assure consumers that they come
from forests that are managed to meet the social, economic and
ecological needs of present and future generations.

Find out more about HarperCollins and the environment at
www.harpercollins.co.uk/green

FT Pbk

For Aidan Hicks

Why should I be out of mind because I am out of sight?
I am waiting for you, for an interval, somewhere very near,
just around the corner. All is well.

(Henry Scott Holland)

The Whole Day Through

EARLY MORNING TEA

Laura had been awake for several minutes before she was aware that there was a problem. She always drew her curtains back just before climbing into bed because she preferred waking early and slowly to daylight than with sudden violence to an alarm. (It was one of the few pleasures of her self-employment as an accountant that, in winter months, she simply started her days later.) So she lay there, entirely comfortable, gently reassembling her sense of where she was and why, catching sweet wafts of the Sombreuil rose that half-obscured her view of the garden and listening to the ravenous cheeping of the blue tit nestlings in the box beside her windowsill. She took in the unsatisfactorily emollient American novel she persisted in reading, then the purple bloom left inside the wineglass she had brought to bed. And her comfort diminished as furniture and pictures reminded her that she was no longer in Paris but in

Winchester, that this was not her room, at least not yet fully her room, but the spare room in her mother's house.

She had just observed, with an unvoiced sigh, that she had been staying in the house long enough now for such a distinction to smack of cowardice, when she realized that the murmuring in the background to the blue tits' noise was not, as she had thought, a collared dove, but Mummy calling her name from the garden.

She swore softly to herself, seeing now that it was still only six-thirty, and went to peer between the rose branches. Then she swore again, less softly, and hurried out, pulling on her dressing gown as she went.

Mummy didn't see her coming and was still calling up at her bedroom window as she emerged, keeping her voice low in an effort not to draw attention from further afield. She was sitting, heavily, inside a rather pretty pink-flowered leptospermum, naked, naturally, and clutching her secateurs in one hand and a Fabian Society mug in the other. She had managed to lose her balance without spilling all the tea and took an absent minded gulp of it as she awaited rescue.

The tableau might have encapsulated the sad decline of a brilliant mind, the pathetic geriatric dementia of the eminent virologist known to her students and peers as Professor Jellicoe. Her mind seemed as sharp as ever, however; only her limbs, not her wits, were failing and her nudity was not a symptom but a decades-old private habit.

Laura's late father had introduced her to naturism early in their relationship and Harriet Jellicoe – Mrs Lewis, as he jokingly called her in conversation with Laura – had practised with a convert's zeal ever since.

'How long have you been stuck out here?' Laura asked her.

'About an hour.'

'Mummy!'

'It's all right. I was only just starting to get a bit cold and only because I'm not moving about.'

'Nothing broken?'

'Just couldn't get up on my own. Bodies are a *bore*!' She continued chatting as Laura offered both arms, cupping Mummy's elbows as Mummy did the same back, sparing them both wrist strain. 'I'd just made myself a cuppa when I saw how that shrubby stock needed cutting back before it set seed then something must have distracted me, a bird or something, and down I went.'

'Come on. Upsadaisy.'

'You'll simply have to put me into a home,' Mummy said as they made their halting progress back indoors.

'We've been through that.'

'Oh yes.'

'You're freezing! Come along. Back to bed for a bit or another cup of tea.'

'More tea, I think. Then I want to get back to that article on bluetongue.'

There was an elegant dressing gown, in sea-green cashmere, kept on the back of the kitchen door in case of unexpected visitors. Laura briskly slipped it over her mother's arms and shoulders and fastened its belt. When she turned back from filling the kettle and lighting a gas ring, Mummy had instinctively shrugged it off.

'Not cold,' she said as Laura made to pick it up. 'Don't fuss so.'

Laura let the garment lie and watched her mother drop violently onto the ancient armchair where she spent much of her day.

Out-manoeuvred into irritable retirement, then imprisoned there by disability, Professor Jellicoe was still able to feel she kept her hand in, as she put it, by two or three compassionate younger colleagues and editors who ensured she was sent articles and books to review. Though largely sedentary, her days were therefore sometimes as full, if not as fulfilled, as when she had headed a research team of her own.

Laura's father, Mr Lewis, had been blithely low-wattage, content always to take second place, and Laura had recently recognized in her own thoughts and behaviour around Mummy distinct traces of his only occasionally mocking respect for her mother's innate superiority. Like him she had become her mother's attendant vestal. Hips, ankles, neck, all might fail in time but were somehow less important than the flame of intellect they supported, which must still be fed and protected for the benefit of all.

This baggily floral throne, with laptop and telephone, printer and Keiller's marmalade jar full of pens and pencils crammed onto a coffee table close at hand, had effectively become Harriet Jellicoe's office, a mahogany invalid table on little wheels, her desk. Assessing the situation soon after moving in, Laura had raised its seat with a stout layer of upholstery grade foam to make it easier for her to sink into but still Mummy could only get out of the thing unassisted by dropping a garden kneeler in front of her, rolling forward to land with her knees on that then clambering her way back to a standing position with the help of other bits of furniture. Before long the chair would have to be replaced with an electrified one that could gently let her down or tip her back out. Laura had brought back brochures from an eager salesman and tried to sell the idea on the basis of how comfortable such chairs were in full reclining mode but Mummy was still powerfully resistant.

'That nasty velour would be sweaty on my skin,' she said. 'I'd never sit in it. It would be a waste of money.'

So for now they made do with the old chair, the garden kneeler and, in case of emergencies, an old china potty discreetly masked by a pile of back copies of *Journal of Virology* (and, increasingly, *Country Life*).

'I pissed in that tea tree,' Mummy observed as Laura set her fresh tea beside her. 'But I don't suppose any harm will come of it. Surprisingly itchy.'

'Just be glad it wasn't a berberis.'

'I'd never plant berberis,' she said hotly, as though the suggestion were demeaning.

'I know,' Laura said. 'I was teasing. Sorry.'

7

Both her mother's gardens had been free of thorns or plants like rue or euphorbia which gave rise to rashes. She made a single exception for roses and these were rarely of the thorniest types and were trained well away from paths or sitting areas.

Laura set the digestives tin on the trolley at Mummy's elbow. 'I'm going back up for a bit,' she said. 'Back soon.'

Mummy had already gone back to her laptop and the latest article for which she was writing a peer review and gave no acknowledgement so Laura slipped out to retrieve the day's newspaper from the big wooden letter box on the back of the garden gate and took that and her own tea back to bed, leaving her to work in peace.

Before all this, years ago it seemed to her now, Laura had been living in Paris in a tiny apartment between the Rue de la Roquette and the Rue du Chemin Vert which she rented very reasonably in return for minor caretaking duties in a grander apartment three floors below which belonged to a largely absentee American ex of hers and his complacent wife.

Whenever fleeting contact with some successful contemporary prompted her to self-analysis, Laura perceived with a flush of feminist shame that her adult life, her life since university, had been mapped out in relationships not achievements. She had always been in work, never gone hungry, which was success of a sort, but work had never been more than a source of rent and food for her and it was a succession of men, not appointments, that came to mind when she pictured her life story.

Already self-employed for some years, in her own peculiar accountancy field, she had moved to Paris at thirty in flight from the aftershocks of an especially misguided relationship with an alcoholic solicitor. In the deluded confidence of love she had believed at first she could save him from himself. When he realized her third attempt to break off with him had succeeded, he tried to take his life. Violently cured of delusion, she was driven away less by any terror of him, though she did fear meeting him without preparation, than by the hurtful condemnation of mutual friends who could not understand the necessity of her not even visiting him in hospital.

In a tiny, rented bedsit with no natural light, she licked her wounds and unexpectedly recovered her self-esteem with Graydon, an American banker who favoured the same little café she did for breakfast and took her on as a sort of challenge because she initially despised him, quite irrationally, for not being French. For nearly a year they had an immensely enjoyable affair, all lust and admiration with courtesy standing in for love.

The affair petered out just when he appeared to be establishing her as an official mistress. His Paris contract was considerably improved on renewal so he bought two apartments in the same building on the fringes of the Marais and persuaded her to move into the smaller one, little more than an extended *chambre de bonne* under the eaves. Even had regularity and domesticity not dimmed their ardour, Graydon brought a subtle, if risky, end to their involvement by introducing Laura to his wife. She liked the wife instinctively, as he surely guessed she would, and gradually realized she preferred lunching with her to sleeping with him. She stayed on in the tiny flat, however, because she still liked them both and they were away so often they needed a care-taker less recalcitrant towards Americans, and with better English, than the building's concierge, someone to take in parcels, oversee decorators or to welcome occasional visitors who rented the bigger apartment in their longer absences.

She had spoken to Mummy regularly – far more so since her widowing – and arranged annual visits in either direction but had maintained a coolly loving distance for the most part, which had suited them both. Mummy wrote, gardened, attended conferences and was in every way the independent, elderly parent of every adult child's dreams. But then she had tripped on a piece of uneven pavement or slipped on a leaf and found herself in hospi-tal with a broken hip.

Only now, far too late in life for much useful treat-ment, did it emerge that she had advanced osteoporosis. This seemed especially cruel since it was usually the scourge of earth mothers, not mothers-of-one. A brace of surgeons pronounced her an unsuitable case for a hip-replacement so her broken bone was merely pinned – a repair that had left her wary and, it seemed, increasingly crippled by pain. When she broke the ankle on the other leg, this time in her thickly screened garden, she lay there overnight and for several hours into a drizzly morning before someone heard her shouting for help.

At that point the permanent return from Paris became inevitable. Arriving at the hospital, Laura had faced a thinly veiled inquisition from a social worker. It wasn't hard to explain how she could be so sure her mother's unsuitable lack of clothes had nothing to do with senile confusion – given her upbringing, Laura was long past embarrassment – but she could tell the young man disbelieved her or was too easily disgusted, for all his training, to find the idea acceptable. She faced a similar problem when she looked into the possibility of retirement housing, even on a short-term basis. Even had Mummy found the prospect bearable, she could not have borne even the most kindly imprisonment if it meant having to wear clothes all day. And Laura doubted whether even Nordic countries had old peoples' homes or sheltered housing where the residents could do the weeding with nothing on.

The facts were cruel in their simplicity: Mummy needed a carer, no one but Laura could fill the role and, as she could do her work anywhere and had no ties, there was no good reason why she should not move in. Not that she *had* moved in. Not properly. Most of her boxed-up belongings remained stacked at the back of the garage, a shadowy and increasingly damp promise that the situation might yet change.

She lost her temper so rarely that the sensation was entirely unfamiliar and felt like the onset of some tumultuous fit or sickness. She was incapable of violence but the social worker, a waxy-haired boy in a shiny suit, was eminently slappable, not least because of the way his intonation rose at the end of every sentence. As he asked his unnecessarily personal questions, he spoke entirely in second-hand phrases so that it was tempting to assume his thoughts were not his own either. She focused on getting through his little grilling as quickly as possible, resisting the impulse to take issue with the necessity of his knowing what she earned or what her mother's marital status was.

'She's single,' she told him.

'Divorced, is that?'

'No. Single. My parents never married. And my father's dead.'

'Ah.'

She watched his fat fist grasp his pen to form the word *widow*. Strictly speaking, an unmarried woman couldn't be a widow, but she let it pass. All that mattered was to get out of his cubby-hole of an office and out of the hospital's stifling atmosphere and, in her indignation, she heard herself telling him things he hadn't even asked and which only taxed his limited understanding and further delayed her escape.

When she finally broke free, having had to agree to an inspection of her mother's house for tripping hazards and other risks that might be modified, she felt her unvoiced anger breaking out at last as a flush on her face and a tremor in her hands and jaw and a sense that everything around her – the visitors with their reused plastic bags, the too chirpy porters, the nurses sullen with exhaustion, the amateur art lining the corridor along which she strode – seemed an affront to her senses.

She had picked up a piece of gravel in her shoe when passing between buildings, which was suddenly digging sharply into her heel. She had paused to pick it out when some man called out her name. She looked around her but took in no faces in the crowd. Then she realized that of course no one knew her here and she had simply over-heard a stranger calling to a different Laura, and this irri-tated her further.

'Laura?' he called again and she turned and saw a handsome man in a suit who was clearly addressing her.

She didn't recognize him at first. In fact she fleetingly mistook him for a BBC foreign correspondent, and wondered how he knew her. He hadn't lost all his hair or become immensely fat but they had not seen each other for over twenty years and the boy had become a man. Hair she remembered as chestnut was now turning grey. But as soon as he smiled she recognized him from the little gap between his front teeth and the way just one cheek dimpled. She recognized, too, the modest way he then gave his name as though she was struggling to place him. She imagined he had a full minute in which to place her before calling out to her.

'Of course!' She laughed. 'It's seeing you so suddenly and out of context,' and they hugged and he kissed her on either cheek then laughed as she automatically moved for a third. 'Oh my God!'

'I know,' he said, pulling back to take her in. 'Twenty years. How did that happen?'

'Stop it,' she said. 'I'm ancient,' but he ignored her, still staring, smiling.

For a second or two they just stared, smiling self-consciously, as each took in the effects of all that time on the other's face. The longer she looked, the more recognizable he became, as though all that time were suddenly nothing. All that mess, the jobs and places and stupid, pointless relationships she hadn't known were pointless at the time; it sprang together like a stretched band suddenly released. Following hard on her anger with the social worker, the sensation left her lightheaded, as if drunk, and she giggled nervously.

'I'd heard you lived in Paris,' he said.

'Well, you're supposed to be in London,' she countered, walking on and drawing him with her. 'I'm visiting my mother. Well, looking after her really.'

'Nothing serious?'

'Broken ankle and a touch of exposure,' she said flippantly. 'General crumble. You know the sort of thing.'

'I'm sorry. I didn't know she lived here.'

'She didn't. I mean, when I ... when we were ...'

'Ah.'

Whenever friends in Paris, women friends, got her talking about past relationships it was always the one with Phil she spoke of as having the most importance, not the earlier one with Ben. The liaison with Phil had been bruising and dramatic and was the reason she had moved to Paris, so naturally it loomed large in her version of herself and her becoming. Brought abruptly face to face with Ben again, she realized, however, that she had been shielding their youthful shared history from scrutiny, perhaps as much to avoid analysing it herself as to protect it from a picking-over and possible belittling by others.

'How about you?' she asked.

'Long story. But I'm working here at the moment.'

'My turn to say "Ah".'

They had reached the door to the car park. There was a cherry tree in blossom nearby and sugar-pink petals had blown into the doorway and been trodden into the doormat like soggy confetti.

Ben stepped to one side and smiled as she turned to look at him. 'It took me a second or two to ...' he began. 'I like you with shorter hair.'

'Thanks. Paris.'

And so, with a married man's confidence, she realized now, he had asked if they could meet again and in a rush she found they were meeting for dinner the following week, once she had got her mother home again and settled back into a routine.

She drank the last of her tea and set her mug with a clink against last night's wineglass. She made herself sit

15

up and start dressing. If she wasn't careful, those few seconds, in which Ben asked her out and looked so becomingly delighted when she said yes, tended to replay themselves in her mind, useless and flattering.

Her eagerness shamed her, naturally. She was no longer a gawky student but a forty-something honorary *Parisienne*, a woman used to men and schooled in sangfroid. A gesture towards cool, even an initial refusal, would have set her value a little higher.

Pants, she told herself. *Bra*. Not long ago underwear had mattered to her and the possibility that someone else might remove it had been reason enough to spend almost as much on it as on the layers that kept it from view. Underwear still loomed large, but now it was her mother's: five extraordinarily expensive pairs of white pants reinforced with hollow plastic hip-armour to prevent breakages. Such was the significance of these garments, so dire the warnings on every side of old women who broke their hips or pelvises and *were never the same again*, that Mummy grew extremely anxious if there weren't at least one pair clean for night-time and one for emergencies. Which meant that laundry was washed and hung out every day rather than just once a week and the gentle knocking together of hip-protectors on the washing line had become as much a part of the garden's sounds as birdsong or wind in the graveyard beeches. Amid such a routine, Laura's handful of elegant, hand-wash-only ensembles had slipped to the back of the drawer in favour of serviceable cotton things – once schoolgirl white – that could be added to the daily washes to help make up a load.

Today's pants, the first to come to hand, were emergency ones from Monoprix, sagging at the waist now, and had turned dispiritingly grey, but no one would know that but her. Which was, she told herself bracingly, a kind of liberation.

MUESLI AND
CHOPPED BANANA

Some time in the early hours, Ben was woken by thumping from Bobby's room – thumping, the sound of a breaking glass or mug, then Bobby's characteristic muddle of swearing and laughter.

'Bob?' he called out. 'Bobby? You okay?'

'I'm fine,' Bobby called back, in their mother's voice, and giggled; then all was quiet again.

Ben had been in the Winchester house for nearly nine weeks now and still found at such moments he was startled afresh to find he was not in bed with his wife but lying alone in another city. He rolled over onto his front, stretching out an arm to where Chloë would have been, and encircled a spare pillow in her stead. The deepest, darkest reaches of the night, when there was least risk of speech, had become the time when his marriage to her felt least insecure.

Then he fell deeply asleep again, worn out by four days of overburdened clinics, and he dreamed of Laura. They were together, back in the amazingly big room she landed in her last year at New College, on the top floor of New Building overlooking a length of the old city wall and Chapel roof and the bell tower. With his adult eyes he saw it and thought, *Christ, what an incredible view!* but he was blasé in the dream, as was she, taking such blessings for granted or as some kind of right won through exams and hard work. But her bed was vast and lapped in linen, like something from a good hotel, not the broken-backed single of reality, so pitiful and noisy they used to pull its mattress onto the floor or simply make love down there, furled in her duvet and getting little friction burns from the nasty nylon carpet.

So there they were, naked and together in her college room with the usual student gestures towards sophistication – a jug of real coffee under one of those horrible paper filter funnels nobody used any more, grapes, brie, a bottle of college port – yet they were their adult selves, he forty-eight to her forty-something, both a bit lived in.

She wasn't beautiful when they were students, not like Chloë, who had notoriously or famously spent her gap year modelling for Ralph Lauren. Even at the time, or especially at the time – with the brutally calibrating eye of untried youth – he looked around and made comparisons and saw that, judged by the accepted norms, Laura was funny-looking, her face on the bony side of feline, her eyes cartoonishly large, her body so boyishly flat and slim it seemed instantly familiar when he first slept with her and lacking in the challenge or mystery he had expected.

Twenty years on she still wasn't exactly beautiful. She had still barely acquired curves but, with maturity, her features were revealed as extraordinary in the way that some actors' were – almost better in close-up, at kissing distance, than when viewed across a room. She had learnt somewhere to present herself differently, so that abrupt verbal shyness was turned to sexy reticence. She had acquired an allure.

But that new, shorter hair she had probably had for years but which still surprised him with the glimpses it gave of her neck was catching the sun and he was hard as anything and just wanted to keep her there or rather to eat her out and fuck her and keep her there because, this being a dream, he was quite without inhibition and they were both so much better in bed than they ever were as students. But she kept pulling away and saying she had to go, she really had to go. That yes, yes, she loved him back and wanted him too, so, so badly and right now but that she really had to go.

Then the alarm went and she said, 'There. You see? The alarm. Now you've made us both late and your wife'll kill us.' Whereupon the alarm went and he woke up with a throbbing groin and a sharp sense of regret.

This was not his room, although he had been sleeping in it for two months. It was his mother's room. He had made changes, done his best to defeminize it with white paint and a purge of her unapologetically trashy taste in fiction. The floral bedspread and cushions had gone to Oxfam. As had the make-up mirror and the lace curtains. But it was still her room, even with a pile of *BMJ*s and *Lancet*s on the bedside table and his shaving things and toothbrush at the grimy edge of the sink.

His own, his old, room, tiny by comparison, had been turned long ago into a sort of snug with the stereo system in it so that their mother could have somewhere to retreat from Bobby when she needed a little peace.

The house had never seemed so small when he was growing up and Bobby was a child, although even then Bobby's clamorous personality had seemed to fill the place. But after his and Chloë's flat on Battersea Park, it felt astonishingly cramped and he appreciated for the first time their mother's sacrifices.

Before Bobby arrived, an unexpected late baby and just possibly a misguided attempt to revive a flagging marriage, she had taught in a good little primary school out in St Cross and their father was a partner in a busy dental practice on St Giles Hill. With Bobby's diagnosis everything changed. She threw in her job to become his full-time speech therapist and carer, saying it was important and they'd cope. Perhaps Father had been leaving her anyway? Perhaps he'd found his second son too overwhelming a disappointment? Perhaps it was just lust? When Ben was twelve to Bob's two, their father announced he was in love with a temporary dental nurse and moving to live with her and her family in Durban. It was, he said, entirely beyond his control.

Ben recalled no fights, no screaming rows, only the sudden disappearance, his mother's explanation and a great, exhausted sorrow. As part of the divorce settlement, their father paid Ben's remaining fees at Pilgrims', the little prep school in the shadow of the cathedral, but he had been living beyond his means and, to avoid picking up a huge mortgage, they were obliged to leave their old house in Edgar Road and move to a gardenless back street in a sad area called Fulflood, on the wrong side of Oram's Arbour, near the station.

Fulflood wasn't a sad area any more. Every house for streets around had been lovingly renovated beyond its original status, every poky yard given a brave Mediterranean makeover. But the house remained small, and back then it must have seemed pretty miserable.

His Friday shirt, the slightly dashing violet one with white stripes, was waiting on its hanger. It wasn't that he had a specific shirt for every day of the week, which would have been really sad, but he always washed his work shirts on a Saturday and ironed them on a Sunday so he was never short of a shirt on a weekday. Which was only slightly sad.

Time to be up. He pulled on his dressing gown and crossed the landing to the bathroom. Bobby was in there, showering, however, which was odd because he always let Ben go in first – it was their established routine as Ben was quicker – and because he hadn't bolted the bathroom door, which was completely out of character.

'Sorry,' Ben called, shutting the door in a hurry. He was sure he had heard him moving around in his room still. But perhaps that was just the radio or noise from the street through an open window. He returned to his room to wait.

He lay down again at first but then worried he might drift back to sleep so he sat on the edge of the bed, put on his reading glasses and caught up with an article on syphilis figures in the under-twenty-fives he had been meaning to read for weeks. He was barely past the opening digest, which was so poorly punctuated he had to read it twice to wring the sense from it, when he heard doors open and close again and hurried out to claim his turn in the shower. His dressing gown fell open disobligingly as he shaved and he felt afresh the unfairness that one's body in dreams seemed to stop ageing at around its twenty-five-year perfection.

The smell of toast and coffee wound up the narrow stairs to greet him. Halfway down he called out, 'You're up bright and early.'

Only it wasn't Bobby at the kitchen table but a stranger about his own age with very black hair, a tattoo and a boxer's nose. He seemed as startled as Ben and slopped his coffee on yesterday's paper. He was what Chloë, with her fearless snobbery, would have called a *Lock-Up-Your-Silver* but there was nothing worth stealing except Ben's car and Bobby's racing bike and Ben saw at a glance that the keys to both house and car were still on their hook and the precious bike was still visible outside the window in their (unimproved) backyard.

'Who the hell are you?' Ben asked without thinking. 'Sorry. I … You startled me. I thought you were Bobby.'

'Mikey,' said the man. 'Mate of Bobby's. Are you Bobby's …?'

'Brother.'

'Brother. Oh. That's okay, then.' He was Irish. He shook Ben's proffered hand uncertainly. Upstairs, doors opened and closed, the lavatory was vigorously used then they heard Bobby's usual tuneless singing from the shower.

'Somebody's happy,' Ben said, pouring himself coffee. 'Have you known Bob long?'

'Yeah,' Mikey said, adding after a pause, 'no. No, actually. He was a Gaydar thing. Look, I've gotta go. Can you tell him I said bye?'

'Sure.'

Mikey stood, tipped the last of his coffee into the sink. 'No rest for the wicked, eh?' he said. 'See you.'

'Yeah. Bye.'

He was plainly left nervous by the encounter as he had trouble opening the front door.

'Press the bottom with your foot as you pull,' Ben called out. 'It's a bit warped.'

The man was released and let himself out with panicky thanks.

Ben fixed himself a bowl of muesli, chopped a banana into it and pondered, as his work constantly invited him to, the vagaries of human innocence. It was a recurrent weakness in the relatives of adults with Down's Syndrome that they preferred not to credit their loved one with a sex drive and were quite capable of treating them as a kind of galumphing child, brimming with love, yes, but only of the nice, innocent kind, like a puppy's, not a man's. Only three weeks ago he had been obliged to explain to a family at his clinic that their little girl, a twenty-five-year-old who had Down's Syndrome, collected biker jackets and was a big fan of Joan Jett and the Blackhearts, was not only HIV positive but had become so through gleeful and repeated unprotected sexual contact.

Bobby didn't have the form of Down's Syndrome everyone thought they knew about. He was one of the rare, arguably luckier ones with the Mosaic variant. In this, through some glitch, not every cell line in his developing zygote had acquired the extra, twenty-first chromosome. (Aged twelve or so, his already biology-mad big brother had made himself an expert in the subject and submitted a project on DNA as part of his scholarship application to Winchester.) Bobby had faced developmental setbacks. He proved slow to walk and was extremely slow to speak. His speech now was mumbling, especially so with strangers. With people he liked, confidence made him positively chatty if not always intelligible. He was shorter than average, had stumpy fingers, was prone to weight gain and had a weak heart. He was more likely to develop leukaemia and had an above-average chance of developing early-onset Alzheimer's. But his looks were unusual rather than characteristic; his tongue was not overly large, his nose and ears not overly small. He had only very slight epicanthic folds to his eyes and from some distant relation he had a shock of white-blonde hair and eyes that really were the colour of cornflowers. As a toddler he had pulled people up short in the street. As an adult, he resembled a young, Chinese-influenced Truman Capote.

And now, at thirty-eight, he finally had a sex life.

For all her furious drive to see that he caught up with his peers as best he could and received a 'normal' education in a city state school, with all the rough and tumble that entailed, their mother had fought shy of making Bobby independent. She loved him too much to let him go and convinced herself he had a better chance of a dignified life at home with her than by taking up the offer of a flat in a purpose-built complex with a warden. And, in truth, Bobby loved her too much to leave even had she encouraged him. They had an intense, battling intimacy – a kind of marriage – that precluded the need for any relationship beyond the home. She returned to teaching, he found the first of a series of undemanding jobs and they continued to be all-in-all to one another until she died. Her death plunged Bobby into such a deep depression that he needed full-time care for a month or two. But it was as though that breakdown had cracked a maternal shell and at last the properly adult Bobby was emerging.

Bobby came down the stairs two at a time. He was fighting with his tie as usual, and as usual Ben had to fight the urge to help him with it. Scorning to wear the ugly synthetic one that was issued by the station management, Bobby had an extravagant collection – one for every working day in the month – and liked to tie them in a Windsor knot worthy of a footballer, but the tying of the knot was a challenge. Shoelaces had always defeated him and he had worn loafers or Velcro-fastened trainers since the fifth form, but he would never accept defeat from a tie.

'You just missed your conquest,' Ben told him and Bobby blushed and turned aside to tear open a bag of the day-old pastries he brought home from work.

'I said he had to clear off straight after his shower,' he mumbled.

'Yes, well, I think he got hungry on the way. Tea?'

'Yeah.'

Ben filled him a mug. Bobby had to serve coffees all day in the station shop and the smell of the drink now sickened him.

'Have you known him long?'

'No. We met on Gaydar. He was minging, wasn't he?'

'Well. I couldn't say.'

'I only meant to have a drink really.' Bobby turned, munching a stale croissant. 'It was a pity fuck.' He swore colourfully as he showered himself with crumbs.

'The term is mercy fuck,' Ben told him, trying not to offend him by laughing.

'Whatever. It's hard to say no,' he said, brushing himself clean.

'Hmm. He said to say bye, anyway.'

'Huh.'

'Heartbreaker.'

'Shut up! He didn't nick any of our stuff, did he?'

'No. Bobs, you were careful, weren't you?'

'Yes.'

'Condoms and stuff.'

'*Yes*,' Bobby growled impatiently and sipped his tea. 'No sex without socks. I'm not a kid.' He tugged back a chair and sat down, slopping his tea, then peeled and ate a banana.

'You're going to be late,' Ben said, glancing at the clock.

'It's fine. Ben?'

'What?'

Bobby scratched himself below the table. 'I think I need to come to your clinic thing.'

'Why? Do you want me to take a look at you?'

'No way!' Bobby was horrified.

'I thought you were careful.'

'I *was*.'

'So, what? Have you got a discharge?'

'Eurggh! No!'

'Soreness?'

Bobby shook his head but he scratched again with the hand that wasn't feeding himself banana.

'Do you itch?' Ben asked.

31

Bobby nodded. 'Started this morning,' he said.

Ben grinned. 'It's crabs, Bob. Pubic lice.'

'It's *really* itchy, though!'

'And it'll get worse, front and back, if you don't sort it. Here.' Ben grabbed one of the free pads they were forever being given by drugs companies and a rival company's pen. 'Go to a chemist on your way to work – that one by the lights'll be open – and ask for a bottle of this. Then you need to go to the Gents and dab it on with loo paper everywhere you itch. Everywhere you've got hair.'

'On my head?'

'Does it itch on your head?'

'No.'

'Fine. Just your pubic hair. Front and back. It burns a bit but it works really fast. We'll need your sheets given a hot wash too.'

'I've not got time.'

'I'll do them. I'm not on till nine-thirty.'

'Oh. Okay. Thanks, Ben.'

'Stop scratching. Eat some toast.'

'No time.' Bobby lurched up and tossed the banana skin into the bin.

'Will I see you tonight?'

'Yeah. It's Shirley's thing then I've got a hot date.'

'Another one? Bobby!'

'Not Gaydar. Proper date. With a meal and everything.'

'Who with?'

'He's a train driver. He's lovely.'

'Oh. Well, we'd better get your little friends sorted.'

'Yeah. Shit. Gotta go.'

'Teeth brushed?'

'Do 'em at work.'

'Phone.'

'Yes. Keys! Yes!' Bobby was halfway to his bike. He stopped, hit his pockets, grinned. 'No.'

Ben picked them off the television and passed them to him.

'I'm not a kid,' Bobby told him.

'You certainly aren't, Master Robert. Go on. Go. Buy that stuff.'

Ben cleared away the breakfast things and went in search of Bobby's sheets. He might be an adult now but he still slept in his boyhood single, watched over by a picture of their mother.

It was a lovely image, entirely spontaneous, snapped by some colleague at her fiftieth birthday party. As a surprise, a gang of friends had taken her and the boys out on the Kennet and Avon Canal for the day. They'd provided a picnic and champagne and even a cake with fifty candles: a day of extravagant pleasure, judged by her careful standards. In the picture she had been persuaded to pose on the boat's roof with her legs dangling – which couldn't have been easy, although she had excellent, if neglected, legs, because she hated being photographed. Just as the shutter was about to click, Bobby had hugged her legs to press a loving kiss on one of her knees. Startled and touched in equal measure, she was laughing at the camera and running a hand through Bobby's snowy hair. She had been so stoical always, so often overburdened and exhausted, never less than loving but often too tired to express it, that it was a delight to see her tricked into revealing this lighter side. Ben too had a copy of the picture somewhere, and they had reproduced it on the order of service for her funeral, but he could never examine it without wondering how differently she might have aged if Bobby had not been born or had been no less healthy, no more demanding than other children. Their father might still have left her and she would have been the same woman, of course, but the emphasis in her character, the distribution of light and shadow, might have been quite different.

Her picture wasn't the only icon above Bobby's bed. His sleep was also watched over by several pin-ups of George Clooney and Tommy Lee Jones and, inexplicably, a ragged magazine clipping of Barbara Castle. Ben didn't snoop but he spotted a couple of discarded condom foils as he stripped the bed, and he was reassured.

The phone rang as he was loading the washing machine and he ignored it, letting his mother's seemingly indestructible old tape-based answering machine take the call. He heard his outgoing message, which Bobby said made them sound like a gay couple short of a social life, and then his wife's voice.

'Oh. Blast. Hello, boys, it's just Chloë. Ben, are you there still? I just wanted a chat about things ...'

He froze, staring down at the answering machine. He could hear Chloë breathing and the click of her car keys as she bounced them nervously in her palm.

'Oh well …' she said. 'I'll try your mobile again. Bye, both.'

He snatched up the phone. 'Chloë.'

'Oh. You are there.'

'Yes. Hi. Sorry. I was just heading out to work.'

'Well, I'll call back on the mobile then you can talk and walk.'

'No. I'll call you. Just give me five minutes to brush teeth and stuff or I'll be late.'

'But will you? Last time you –'

'Yes, yes. I'll call. Promise. Five minutes.' He hung up and realized his heart was racing.

If only she had become a monster, it would be so much easier. Weirdly, however, she had been far closer to monstrous when he was first in love with her. When they first met, her values were all awry, she was laughably vain and full of politically unsound received opinions dressed up as pretty ignorance. But physically she was perfection, with flawless skin, a cascade of tawny blonde hair, big grey eyes that spoke at once of sorrow and invitation. She was the same age as the other girls in her year but was so groomed and poised by comparison, so careful, that she had all the charisma of an older woman with none of experience's taint.

It was a secret relief to discover she wasn't both a model *and* an intellectual. Ben was such a tunnel-visioned scientist at this stage that all the humanities students seemed clever to him because they were cultured and studied the sort of things that enlivened conversation rather than the reverse. Chloë was no exception – reading French – and it was only after a few conversations that he realized she had only made it into Oxford by virtue of the efficient cramming methods at her boarding school, not from any originality of thought or even hunger to learn. Off the leash from her schoolmistresses, she had been mentally dawdling since her first-year exams, shamelessly pillaging swottier students' notes and essays, and would be lucky if she scraped a third.

He had noticed her around the college – how could he not? – but had been content to marvel at her from a distance, assuming she was neither single nor attainable.

Being drawn into her orbit was as disorienting as being unexpectedly taken up by someone famous. The glamour of her turned his head. At a time when most female students, Laura included, were *women*, politically, her femininity undid him. And there was a no less disgraceful pleasure in having a girl all other men wanted. Her attractions were entirely external, or to do with how other people responded to her. If, as their relationship progressed, her words and deeds revealed less appealing aspects, he found he could overlook them as one could overlook the health implications of food or drink that was especially delicious.

In some terrible way, however, as their marriage had matured, it was as though she had sensed the snail's pace withdrawal of his love for her and, suffering for it, became a better person by barely detectable degrees. She still had no sense of humour, especially at her own expense, but she now strove to understand the things she had once dismissed. She had distanced herself from her father's political savagery and smothering daddyism and, through her voluntary work at a special school, acquired a raft of new friends the old (or rather, younger) Chloë would not have spoken to. His dealings with her now were shot through with a guilty evasiveness she would once have found deeply suspicious but now met with loving concern.

'If I met her for the first time today,' he thought, as he shut the front door and found her smiling face on his mobile's screen and tapped it with a little wand, 'we might even become friends.'

'Hello,' he said when she answered. 'I'm back. How are things?'

He disliked walking and talking at the same time because it played havoc with his concentration and made him all too likely to say something foolish or unguarded. He had plenty of time so he walked only as far as the unfenced sloping park called Oram's Arbour and sat on a still dewy bench there.

Chloë talked about her school work, which she loved, and her merchant bank job, which she had come to hate and how the school had once again offered her a paid, full-time position. She was dithering about whether to take it. She went on to tell him about a Sunday lunch party given by friends she thought of as theirs but who were hers, all hers, people who intuitively disliked him and were probably hoping his absence would become permanent so they could reassert their influence and say they told her so.

'You're not listening,' she said suddenly and he realized he wasn't and that it was suddenly later than he thought. 'I am,' he insisted, jumping up and continuing on his way up Step Terrace towards the hospital.

'Ben, I have to ask you something.'

'What?'

'Is there someone else?'

'How do you mean?' he asked, horrified, stalling as he so often did with her by feigning an absent mind.

'How do you fucking think?' she snapped and she sniffed deeply and he realized she was either crying already or fighting tears.

He pictured the angry gesture with which she'd be dragging away a tear with the back of her spare hand – angry yet not so violent as to dislodge a contact lens.

Over the last two years he had often considered the possibility of breaking up with her. Three kindred inhibitions always stayed his hand. There was reluctance to hurt her and guilt that she thought he was a better man than he was. Lastly he was paralysed by self-disgust at the knowledge that, deep down, he did ever so slightly despise her for not being clever enough.

'Have you met someone new?' she asked.

He snatched at the opening this offered him, despising his cowardice. 'No,' he said, now picturing Laura as a student whom he had known longer than he'd known his wife. 'There's no one new. Darling, we need to talk –'

'I hate it when you call me that.'

'Sorry. Sorry. But this isn't the time. Not if I'm racing to work.'

She sniffed again. He heard the thunk of her wedding ring against her phone's mouthpiece. 'When, then? Tonight?'

He thought, remembered the funeral. 'No. I've got to go out with Bobby straight after work.'

'The weekend?'

'Okay. Yes. Let's agree to speak over the weekend.'

'Sorry I shouted,' she said.

'Don't be silly. Sorry to be so provoking.'

'I love you, Ben,' she said.

And the most honest he could be was to say simply, 'I know,' before he hung up.

BREAKFAST

Stewed apricots or prunes with home-made yoghurt, wholemeal toast, thick downland honey and coffee. Laura had long since adopted the Parisian way of eating next to nothing for breakfast but preparing the meal for her mother every day had slowly seduced her into sharing it. Unless Mummy had passed an especially bad night it was one of the more cheerful of the day's feasts; the unvarying menu lacked shocks or disappointments, the conversation was light, spiced by small notes of optimism, buoyed up by the carefully maintained pretence that they were both still in a position to lay plans.

'I was thinking I'd move that camellia by the water butt,' her mother would say. 'Or dig it up altogether. It's not really singing for its supper and the new growth has that nasty vomitty pink tinge to it.'

Or they would discuss some play or exhibition reviewed in that day's paper and agree they *ought* to go and see it, while doing nothing so rash as to make a specific arrangement to do so.

The arrival of letters provided much fodder. Professor Jellicoe had always received invitations to conferences or lectures, and to school reunions or hospital or university fundraising events, but the flow of these, it seemed to Laura, was less impressive than it had been, as though it was finally dawning on the senders that her mother now rarely said yes. She remained meticulous in always writing to say no, however, 'So they know I've still got a pulse,' she said, and, presumably, because the invitations represented at least a trickle of continuing professional recognition.

Of far more interest now were the nearly daily catalogues – Mummy having discovered with disability the pleasures of home shopping. Leaving butter smears and crumbs on the pages, they would pick through arrays of slippers and gloves, thermal underwear, birdseed, cut-price cashmere and ingenious domestic gadgets with interest, though ordered only rarely.

'I've just bought twenty kilos of songbird crumble and a box of dried eelworms. Why on earth do they think I'd want to order more right away?'

Laura received announcements of births and invitations to significant birthday parties. All her friends in the market for doing so had either married or put all expectations behind them. Invariably she received work correspondence: letters from Revenue and Customs or fat padded envelopes of receipts and explanation.

Mummy tended to be the one who received *real letters*, possibly because she was the one who still wrote them. A fluent Internet user for professional communication, she resisted the lazy attractions of personal e-mail. She never tired of pointing out how many of her friends had died yet she maintained astonishingly regular contact with two pen pals she had been writing to since girlhood, one in Sweden, one in Canada. Anna-Birgit, the Swede, was a farmer's widow, Joyce, the Canadian, a housewife who made a lot of jam and bred Shelties. Were the three women to be brought together they would have even less common ground socially than when they were uniformed schoolchildren but they had been writing to one another for so long that, on paper at least, time and ageing itself had become the territory they patrolled together. Laura had grown up with regular bulletins from these correspondents and had recently enjoyed catching up with them as with some ancient, undemanding soap opera. Neither woman was a wit or even a prose stylist but the simple longevity of each correspondence lent the death of a favourite cow or gathering of a troublesome but long endured neighbour all the quality of high drama.

Today, however, the only breakfast interest was a holiday postcard from Polteath whose signature neither of them could decipher. Mummy could think of no one who had said they were due to go to Cornwall and decided it must be from someone she hardly saw any more – some second cousin – who wrote out of duty, not affection.

'The great thing with holiday postcards is one doesn't have to answer them,' she said, when they had done deciphering. 'So it couldn't matter less,' and she set the card on the little shelf above the kitchen table where they could admire its image of cliffs and sand and improbably blue sea.

'Falls Clinic at eleven-thirty,' Laura reminded her, topping up their coffee.

'Bugger,' Mummy said and tore the plastic wrapping off an old girls' journal from St Swithun's she had been avoiding for two days.

They had only once holidayed on a beach – when they took tents and camped at Espiguette, just outside Aigues Mortes. Otherwise they had returned year after year to the same naturist holiday camp in Dorset.

Summerglades. The place was so deeply embedded in Laura's memories, and she had been so small when she first experienced it, that she only had to hear or read the word *glade* or even *summer* to feel softened pine needles underfoot or to smell the rotten sweet scent of lake water drying on her skin.

It had been a working farm for centuries, one that happened to have a wooded valley at its heart and a long, unevenly-shaped lake created by the partial damming of the stream at the valley's bottom. Then an inheriting son had a revelation when honeymooning in Bavaria in the 1920s and created a holiday camp where visitors were encouraged to leave off their clothing for the duration of their stay.

Guests were housed in a sprinkling of simple wooden chalets beneath the trees. There was a shower block for women and girls and one for boys and men, a recreation hall (a Nissen hut with a gym at one end and chairs and tables at the other) and a restaurant-cum-dance hall (also a Nissen hut, but with better furniture). One could walk in the woods, swim in the lake, row or sail on it, ride bicycles along trails about the wood or simply sit in the sun. Simply sitting was rarely a popular option since even on a hottish day in a sheltered valley the blissfully naked needed motion to avoid becoming chilled. The resident games master and mistress organized sporting activities several times a day. Riding, rounders, tennis-ball cricket and badminton were popular. And since guests tended to arrive and leave on Saturdays, a ferociously competitive tournament was held every Friday afternoon – a naturist school sports day – with sack and three-legged races, egg and spoon races, rope climbing, swimming contests and an obstacle course (on which most children gained the upper hand by play-practising all week).

In the evenings, as was only practical after nightfall, families dressed for dinner after which there was usually dancing, to a free jukebox, but sometimes a talk with slides from one of the guests. The latter varied from the scholarly – ornithology, botany and ancient civilizations were perennial favourites – to less highbrow, often unintentionally comic screenings of holiday slides and cine-films.

There was no church – a thing that had initially attracted Laura's Fabian grandparents to the place – but every Sunday saw a few worshippers slipping out of the place for an hour or two, uneasy, even shifty, in suits and hats.

Any queasiness Laura felt about Summerglades was retrospective. She had no unhappy memories of it. A life-time habitué, thanks to said grandparents, her father introduced her mother to the place – and to naturism – soon after they met, and took Laura there twice a year from babyhood, so that she grew up with the same warmly proprietorial feelings about it that wealthier children displayed towards holiday cottages in Cornwall or villas in Provence. Most small children delighted in raucous nudity and she had never forgotten the feral pleasure of running free in the woods in a naked gang, becoming streaked with mud and grass and puddle water and it not mattering. The principal vindication of naturism, her father always maintained, was the curing of prudery and prurience, and in this he was correct. Entirely used to all ages and shapes of nakedness from infancy, she was not only unselfconscious but unjudgemental. Ugly clothes revolted her, ugly people never did. Faced with bodies that were large or old or in any way unusual, she met them with a neutrality that caused consternation among her friends in France, for whom bodily elegance – as much as sartorial chic – was seen almost as a civic duty.

Puberty was the only time she remembered being uncomfortable at the camp. She spent two consecutive trips there outlandish and sullen in a one-piece swimming costume, but that was because she was menstruating and lacked the courage of those women, nicknamed *teabaggers* by her feral friends, who never let this bother them. She felt no shame at emerging breasts or hair and had been stealing fascinated glances at older girls and boys for years so was quite prepared, and even a little proud, when the changes happened to her.

If anything, Summerglades made her uncomfortable elsewhere. It was only a man-made Eden, of course, and not without serpents – affairs erupted, marriages foundered and, just occasionally, there were other people's fathers or brothers who stared or were too keen on contact sports. But these last were easily laughed at or reported which, like open-air sex or even heavy petting, resulted in prompt and unconditional banishment. She realized now that their holidays there were not just the one time her parents set aside their work and students to be entirely focused on familial pleasures but must have been one of the few occasions when they had actively pretended to be married. Unmarried men over eighteen were barred from Summerglades and so, after two unfortunate incidents – one with *Health and Efficiency* magazine, one with a Soho cinema – were cameras of any sort.

Looking back, as she stared at the mysterious Cornish postcard, Laura realized neither parent had instructed her in the matter. She had known instinctively that naturism would not be understood by her friends at school.

She was never told it was dirty or something to be ashamed of but there must have been an implicit instruction that theirs was an innocent pleasure not everyone would understand or appreciate. On every trip to Summerglades they would make fully clothed excursions *back into the textile world*, as her father put it, to visit castles and villages, churches and tea rooms. The Instamatic camera hidden in the glove compartment would be retrieved and photographs would be taken on these occasions which went into an album to form an official or alternative holiday narrative. They were good excursions, as enjoyable as they were instructive, but because of the donning of clothes they involved, they inevitably felt like interruptions of the holiday proper, and the small shelf of albums to which they contributed seemed an imperfect if not exactly hypocritical record.

Self-sufficient in their pseudo-marriage, her parents were the sort of people who had colleagues rather than friends. They often left their clothes off around the house and garden, at least at weekends. They had no naturist friends and neither did Laura, apart from the small gang with whom she joined up at Summerglades, which meant that any entertaining involved the selection of clothes and a sense of the family making an effort to pass for normal. The strain this involved inevitably meant that colleagues or school friends were rarely invited twice.

Laura grew to be self-contained. An early school report pronounced *Lara keeps her own counsel.* (She was Lara then, named for the passionately divided heroine of

Pasternak's celebrated novel, but grew so sick of having 'Lara's Theme' sung at her in school that she acquired a U at the first opportunity.) She maintained a wall of privacy about her family life as impenetrable as her parents' escallonia hedges. But she also fell into an early habit of keeping her own life private from her parents and to this day there was much about her that her mother didn't know. She never thought of this as secrecy but as dignity: the maintenance of a kind of order. Now that they were living in close proximity again she took pains to respect her mother's privacy whenever practicable and trusted that the courtesy was mutual.

As to the effect of her parents' naturism on her love life, it had left her happy in her skin, dauntingly unselfconscious about removing her clothes. It had also robbed naked flesh of any power to excite her. For her, eroticism was found at the body's periphery: in clothes, in scents, in the sound of a man's voice. She made love, Graydon the banker told her, like a blind woman.

There was a death announced in the old girls' magazine which had passed her mother by and which demanded tribute. She fell to writing a belated condolence letter while Laura cleared the breakfast things away and loaded the dishwasher.

'Do you want a hand getting dressed later?' she asked.

'I'll be fine,' Mummy said, frowning at her writing pad.

FILTER COFFEE

Ben took another mouthful of the staffroom's filter coffee and winced. Stewing quietly on its hotplate all morning had done nothing for its complex flavours. He moved over to the sink to pour the rest away then stepped outside onto the fire escape for a few lungfuls of relatively fresh air before guilt tugged him back inside and to his next patient.

Butterfield's original 1863 County Hospital, a first cousin to the Natural History and Pitt Rivers museums, might have been placed high on a hill for the health benefits of uncontaminated breezes but it also lay pointedly outside the old city limits, on land once set aside for life's undesirables: prisoners, plague pits, the dead and the infectious. In what felt like a hangover from Edwardian practice, the centre for genito-urinary medicine, known invariably as the GUM clinic, was housed in a grim redbrick house quite separate from the main hospital campus. It lay on a stretch of the Romsey Road where the pavement was oppressively narrow, and was hemmed in by a full graveyard, heavy traffic and the jail.

As he climbed the hill to work, Ben had soon learnt to spot the freshly released prisoners on their way to the train and coach stations since they tended to be carrying their few personal possessions in tell-tale transparent plastic bags. Building plots in the city centre had grown so scarce, property prices so absurdly high, that there was talk of the prison being converted to luxury flats; the oldest part was a listed building, after all, and granted grim immortality as the spot where Hardy's Tess was hanged for murder. Yet it was hard to imagine the citizens of such a prosperous place consenting to the erection of a new prison anywhere that wasn't out of sight and preferably with a reassuringly remote postcode.

Like a Victorian school, the GUM clinic fell into male and female halves, each with its own waiting room and with the staffrooms as a shared territory in between. Although he had briefly visited a female clinic during his houseman years, when he was closely chaperoned, patients preferred to be seen by doctors and nurses of their own gender and the preference was echoed among the staff. Ben wasn't sure – he was a poor judge – but he believed most of his male GUM nurses were gay and gathered, from unguarded comments in the common room and loos, that some of them assumed he was too.

Back at his desk, he glanced at the next pseudonym listed on his computer then opened his consulting room door and looked at the group of men dotted around the waiting area.

'Bruno?'

A thin, dark-haired man stood up and made a faint, waist-height gesture with his hand. He was dressed as if for a job interview.

'Hello,' Ben told him. 'This way.' He shut the door behind them. 'Take a seat,' he said and sat himself, as trained, beside his desk not behind it. 'It's your first time here, I think.'

'Yes.' He was about Bobby's age, possibly younger.

'Well, as the receptionist will have explained, your being here and whatever we do for you remains entirely confidential. So don't worry that anything you tell me will get back to your employer or doctor or anyone else. What can I do for you?'

'I've developed a ... a discharge.'

'Yes?' Ben hoped he was looking encouraging.

'In front.'

'Right. And discomfort with it?'

'It hurts when I piss.'

'And when did this start?'

'Two, no, three days ago.'

'And when did you last have sex?'

It was always *have sex* not *make love* because the less emotive phrase encouraged candour. He had colleagues who preferred *fuck*, but when he said it it felt artificially coarse.

'At the weekend,' the man told him. 'At a conference.'

'Was this a regular partner?'

'No. A girl, another delegate.' Ben met the man's eye encouragingly then cast a practised glance down at his wedding ring. 'My partner doesn't know.'

Ben paused in his note-taking. 'And have you not had sex with her since the weekend – with your regular partner?'

'It's a he. Er, no. I mean, we've shared a bed obviously, because we live together, and hugged a bit but we haven't …'

'Made love,' Ben supplied, because these small touches of mischief made the work bearable.

'No,' the man said and flushed.

'Right. Well, good. That's one less problem you have to deal with! And when you do have sex with him, do you wear condoms?'

'No.'

'Why not?'

The man reddened even more. 'We're faithful. As a rule.'

'Of course you are. And when you have sex, or make love, do you have anal intercourse?'

'Usually.'

'Do you penetrate him?'

'No. No. He fucks me usually.'

'I see. Right then, Bruno, we'd better give you a thorough checking-over. If you'd like to step in here.'

There were tiny treatment rooms to either side, to which the nurses had independent access. Ben showed

58

Bruno into one then asked him to remove his suit and to lower his pants. He donned a pair of latex gloves and examined his penis and scrotum, gently pulling back the foreskin to check for paraphimosis and looking into the meatus to note the discharge, which was still fairly watery. He also checked for lice or scabies, or any lumps or warts. Luckily Bruno was not one of the patients – straight or gay – who became uncontrollably excited at the touch of latex or by the mere act of being examined. Ben had never quite decided how to deal with these. Obviously a polite show of indifference was called for, since anything else might prove disastrous, yet a complete lack of acknowledgement always seemed a little discourteous. Once one prodigiously well endowed patient divined his dilemma and had overcome his own embarrassment sufficiently to say,

'You could always applaud.'

As was usually the case among GUM patients, Bruno smelled strongly of soap. The countless dinner-table grillings Ben had faced about his work over the years tended to involve an assumption that his patients were unclean, and he always felt honour bound to explain that shame or a compensatory sense of decorum meant that most of them arrived for their appointments scrupulously, and recently, washed, often sporting slightly inflamed patches from where they had just been rubbing and scrubbing.

Men at dinner parties and, less often, women wanted to know if the penises he encountered were ever spectacularly large or grotesquely small and he could honestly reassure them that most, funnily enough, were average, neither pitiful nor frightening. But occasionally he liked to shame the prurient by pointing out that men with extremely small endowments were far less likely to show up in a clinic for sexually transmitted disease since people were far less likely to sleep with them and a horror of ridicule was, in any case, quite likely to have put them off sex.

Ben then had Bruno lie on his side on the couch and draw up his knees so that he could check internally for any abnormalities. On withdrawing his finger he glanced down to check for blood traces before discarding the gloves.

'Right, Bruno. Don't worry. Nothing sinister. Stay as you are and a nurse will come in next to take a quick swab front and back and in your mouth and to take some blood. He'll knock first so as not to startle you. He'll also want you to give a urine sample – you'll be left on your own to do that, don't worry. We'll be checking for your urinary PCR – looking for traces of viral or bacterial activity. And the smears will let us do a pus cell count under a microscope. We'll check you for hepatitis A and B as a matter of routine but would you like an HIV test while we're at it? I need your legal permission for that.'

Bruno had sat up on the edge of the couch and preserved his modesty with his shirt tails. 'You mean like for AIDS?'

Ben nodded. 'Uh-huh.'

'No thanks.'

'Certain?'

'Definitely.'

'Right you are. And finally if, as seems likely, you have picked up an infection we'll obviously be able to treat you but we need to do all we can to stop the infection spreading. Is there any way you could contact or enable us to contact the girl at the conference? We could do it anonymously.'

'No,' Bruno said, worried. 'No way. Sorry but, well, I don't even know her name or who she works for.'

'Shame. Maybe she'll come in on the other floor under her own steam. So. When the nurse is through with you you'll need to wait back in the waiting area until your results are ready. Or make an appointment to come back but it's best we treat you today, obviously.'

'Will it be long?'

'Half an hour, if you're lucky. See you later, then.'

An earlier patient's test results had come through while he was with Bruno. He returned to the waiting area and called for Tim. Two men stood.

'Sorry,' Ben added. 'Tim 1972.'

From nine-thirty until shortly before he broke for lunch, Ben examined thirty penises and eight back passages. Six of the back passages were gay, one was 'bi-curious' and the last was straight but so convinced *something had happened* on a camping trip, despite medical appearances to the contrary, that Ben referred its owner for counselling.

All the men who consulted him were carrying one of the usual venereal infections, apart from one of the two who had been sent in for an all-clear before their new girlfriends would sleep with them. And these, depressingly, were the only ones all morning to request tests for HIV.

People attending the GUM clinics presented a human Venn diagram that varied little from day to day except in its occasional startling particulars. One of that morning's patients had gone down on a woman with such zeal he had managed to pick up a pubic lice infection in his eyebrows. Another had neglected his gonorrhoea for so long that the pus he was producing actually was the green of everyone's worst imaginings rather than the usual mundane off-white.

Genito-urinary medicine was probably the medical field with the least variety in the presenting cases and the most patients convinced that their case was especially shameful or revolting. It was the dullest, medically, but one of the richest in psychological interest. This was not his specialism of choice – his favoured area was the treatment of patients with HIV, but clinics for the two still tended to be administratively, if not physically, linked, both to save money and because, in terms of preventative medicine, they had ground in common.

As a medical student it was virology that captivated him and he nursed dreams of devoting a career to research in the field, finding a cure to something elusive or at least the genetic key that would pave the way to such a breakthrough. His houseman year was spent at what was then St Stephen's Hospital in Chelsea and he found himself assigned to the Thomas Macaulay Ward just as the first wave of London's AIDS cases was being admitted. The shock of patients having to be treated for a syndrome for which there were then few hard and fast treatments on a ward which had to be kept locked yet even so was plagued by journalists trying to bluff their way in and photographers aiming telephoto lenses from fire escapes in search of a ghoulish scoop woke him from the long sleep of medical study and he was startled by a clinical vocation. Not even HIV research – however well paid and glamorous by comparison – could beat the fulfilment he found in battling to prolong and then to save lives in medical territory that was still drawing up its own maps.

Chloë's father was a heart specialist. Brutally unin- quisitive, dismissive of the world beyond his operating theatres, he had never recovered from his disappoint- ment that not one of his three children, all daughters, had proved studious enough or sufficiently scientific to follow him into medicine. Chloë was the hardest-work- ing and had at least made it to Oxford, but he'd discounted French as *a girl's subject*, at which she'd merely exclaimed, 'Dad!' and laughed. She won some favour with him, however, by delivering him a medical son-in-law. Though common decency prevented him saying so in public, he was disgusted at Ben's wilfully steering his career into what he saw as a professional dead end and at first his dismay was dutifully echoed by Chloë.

Thanks to the examples of Hollywood and European royalty, however, AIDS and its related charities became fashionable for a while and Chloë found a way to make the situation work for her. Through her connections she had walked into a job in a merchant bank. In her free time, though, she took part in fundraisers, she volunteered as a driver for patients and she gave up every fourth Saturday to work for the AIDS equivalent of meals-on-wheels. But then the predicted holocaust failed to materialize, at least among the moneyed white, and the charities shifted their focus as Ben's wards were filled with less easily huggable sufferers, increasingly refugees – many of them conflict-numbed rape victims from Rwanda, Zimbabwe and Sudan and their infected babies – and drug addicts, who the volunteers had to learn to call drug users.

But in a way Ben would never have predicted, Chloë discovered that she liked being involved on more than just a fundraising level. She liked getting her hands dirty, at least metaphorically. She enjoyed the unpredictable human contact. Whether this was because she was developing a taste for doing good or simply that she was discovering there was a pleasure to be had in goading her father, he couldn't have said.

The turning point came when St Stephen's was closed for its grand rebuilding as the Chelsea and Westminster. While Ben and his patients were temporarily rehomed,

Chloë startled him by negotiating only part-time employment at the bank so as to volunteer two days a week at a school for the mentally disabled – a Special School – in Wandsworth. Banking was boring, she said. She had enjoyed her contact with the children on the ward and wanted something more challenging in her life. They could cope financially – her mother had bought them the flat as a wedding present – and the new work, which could turn into a career if she decided to take some formal training and commit to it, made her happier and easier to live with.

What neither of them had foreseen was the hunger it stirred in her for motherhood. From the day they met she had always been meticulous in her birth control, adamant that the thought of motherhood repelled her. This had saddened him a little at first but only because it felt like a rejection of him but he had long since grown not just used to the idea but secretly relieved by it. Perhaps it wasn't as much of a volte-face as it seemed? Perhaps she had been becoming broody for years but not admitting it to herself?

Had she simply become pregnant the usual way, unexpectedly and without advance discussion or planning, their marriage might have trundled on in its uneventful, unsurprising way. Her coming off the pill had seemed so dramatic. They had actually celebrated it and convinced themselves a pregnancy would make itself known in a matter of weeks. But with each month that passed, each disappointing period, the matter changed from ground for joy to being a subject best avoided. At last she submitted to some tests and found she couldn't conceive, or not easily. Given the high failure rate in couples over forty, the doctors they saw were actively discouraging about their seeking IVF.

Inspired by days spent with some of the more beguiling toddlers at the Special School, Chloë then hit on the idea not just that they should file for adoption but that they should actively seek to adopt a baby with what were euphemistically called special needs. She was tenacious and pursued the idea alone, finding out all the details, littering the normally tidy flat with pamphlets and forms. And, all unwittingly, she brought Ben to the shocking realization that he didn't want to have a child with her, still less adopt one. Passion had cooled, as passion did, but he assumed that love, a steady, undramatic kind of love, would take its place. Had he loved her, he would surely have wanted to raise a family with her. He would surely at least have masked his lack of enthusiasm so as to make her happy. Instead he found he couldn't pretend. He found a way through the situation, of course, protesting that they could find another specialist, both have more tests, that they could even investigate getting IVF privately. And he told her that a disabled child would be so demanding she would have to give up everything else she liked doing.

'Think of my mum,' he told her. 'Think of Bobby.'

'I am thinking of Bobby,' she countered. 'Bobby's lovely.'

So now he felt even guiltier, for not only did he not love his beautiful wife but he appeared to be retrospectively rejecting his own brother.

On and off, for what felt like weeks, they argued in exhausting circles until sometimes it seemed to Ben that she too had sensed what the situation had revealed about his feelings towards her and was goading him to a confession. The more opposition she faced – and in a rash moment he had drawn her parents into the discussion, so the opposition was considerable – the more determined she became until her simple faith in the rightness of what she wanted them to do and their ability to do it came to seem almost religious.

Relief arrived from an unexpected quarter when his mother grew sick. No one had expected her to die. She developed ovarian cancer. She had an ovarectomy and hysterectomy and underwent chemotherapy, which appeared to have worked. But then the cancer recurred, this time in her spine, and, still weakened by treatment of the initial outbreak, she declined further intervention and deteriorated and died with bewildering speed.

Diverted from their own cares, both Chloë and Ben visited the sad little household regularly throughout her illness and the aftermath of her death, Ben often electing to stay for weekends because Bobby was so miserable. It soon became apparent that Bobby could not cope without his mother or was too depressed to try. They fixed him up with care workers to call in every day to see how he was, to check he was eating and cleaning properly, but he hated that and wouldn't let them in half the time. So, egged on by Chloë, whose bank had made major donations to the place, Ben took him on a trial visit to a residential community in Devon, a sort of village where people with Down's Syndrome and other learning challenges were supposed to enjoy a kind of idyllic independence farming and making pots and rugs. But Bobby fled back to Winchester in days, saying he hated the country, loathed handicrafts and didn't see why he should be *stuck with a load of mongs*. And once again he showed every sign of depression, not eating, not getting up, not showing up for work and even getting repeatedly drunk and abusive.

There seemed no choice left them, since Bobby vociferously refused to be prised out of his childhood home again, even to join Chloë and Ben in London, and Ben had moved to join him in Winchester until the crisis had passed and a long-term solution could be found. At first he commuted, living with Bobby in Winchester and catching a daily train, Tube and bus to the Chelsea and Westminster, but a couple of daytime crises, the second of which involved a clumsy overdose of aspirins, convinced him to take the Winchester job so he could be never more than fifteen minutes from his brother's side.

Chloë claimed she understood but there was an obdurate quality to her acceptance. She did not offer to come with him and when, a little late, he suggested she could, that they could let the flat to cover the costs of commuting, she only said a sad, 'Well, let's see.'

She had visited him a few times and he had visited her but it was so horrible that suddenly it felt like just that – *visiting* – not like the simple resumption of married continuity. His mother's house was so small and there was so little privacy with Bobby about the place. The last time he slipped up to London for a weekend they had hideously unsuccessful sex (definitely *not* lovemaking) after which he actually found himself weeping in the bathroom. They had been so studiously considerate towards one another, so cheerily evasive, in the hours that were left them, that he could barely wait to get away again. It was as though there was a dead thing in the flat with them and they were each avoiding raising the subject of its smell.

In the name of brotherly love, Ben had taken a large pay cut, going from being an HIV consultant in the Chelsea and Westminster to a staff grade GUM and HIV doctor saddled with a level of donkey work in overburdened clinics of a kind he had not known in years. He had dimly hoped some kind of mutual transfer might be negotiable – a temporary one, of course; he clung, for Chloë's sake, to the idea that all this upheaval was temporary – but Winchester was a desirable posting because of the good schools and, as yet, there were no senior vacancies, even temporary ones.

He had slowly helped Bobby back to stability, helped him find a new job, broadened his horizons by buying him a computer, installing a Wi-Fi system in the house and teaching him how to use them both. He had unwittingly shown him the way to the mixed delights of online gay dating but was now beginning to wonder whether he had not wrought a subtler change simply by offering masculine company to a man too long boyed by his mother.

Chloë had visited just once since the bad sex episode. Bobby adored her and she was amused by him in short measures, although Ben suspected her brother-in-law's late-flowering sexuality was something she found hard to stomach. When Bobby was out of the way, she had once again raised the adoption question and, instead of arguing, Ben had found himself shrugging and saying,

'It'll be your child. You must do what you think right.'

His tone of weary defeat, even apathy, had startled her into friendly evasion, as the bad sex had before, and they had both almost fallen on Bobby with gratitude when he returned to divert them.

Ben had just begun to admit to himself that he was happier away from Chloë than with her but that Bobby was no longer sufficient excuse for their living apart when he ran into Laura in the hospital.

ELEVENSES

While the days remained warm enough, Laura maintained a little office for herself in the summerhouse at the far corner of the garden. Her mother had only ever used it as a potting shed and, unlike Laura's father, had never been a tidy shed keeper. Spades and forks were jumbled together with all a keen gardener's practical detritus: tangles of tar scented twine, stakes, some still with snail shells on the top to protect the gardener's eyes, seed trays, sacks of compost, sand and vermiculite and an insane quantity of plastic flowerpots. Her mother seemed to have passed beyond the stage of doing much propagation so Laura had cleared and wiped the home-made kitchen table from her childhood, one of several bits of furniture her father had built, which stood by the summerhouse window and swept away several generations of corpse-heavy cobwebs from the glass. It made a pleasant, fair weather work space, removed from the distractions of the house but not so far that she wouldn't know if Mummy got into trouble.

Her father had never lived in Winchester – this was the house Mummy bought after his death – but the shed reminded Laura of him, not just its scents of creosote and earth and seaweed fertilizer but her mother's cavalier way with precious tools, which he would have itched to tidy. He had been dead over ten years now but still she felt she had not mourned him as she ought. Possibly this was because Mummy had required so little of her in the weeks after his death, had made no consoling demands. Possibly it was because Laura had been living in Paris at the time, in a place not associated with him. But now she was forever being surprised by memories of him or stumbling on things unexpectedly associated with him and trying Mummy's patience with her insistence on discussing minute details of the distant past.

She had never planned to become an accountant and still hesitated to call herself one since what she did felt like little more than bookkeeping. She had read maths at Oxford but made a mess of her finals, then rather lost her way in life. Short of money at the end of a long spell of erratic temping, she drifted into a job that involved bookkeeping and found she took a certain cool pleasure in it. She was put through accountancy exams by the firm she worked for and passed them easily, but she disliked corporate life. Contemporaries who had ended up in more artistic jobs, as chaotically freelance journalists, graphic designers, decorators and novelists, began paying her to do their accounts and tax returns for them. Soon they had recommended her to enough friends and colleagues that she found she could leave the tedious firm and work for herself with only a small loss of income. In London then Paris she proceeded to make a living in a way she could never have foreseen. E-mail and online tax returns had freed her, more than ever, to work wherever she chose to live.

She specialized in hopeless cases – the sort of people who hid their bank statements unopened behind the breadbin and couldn't work out a simple percentage even on a calculator, had they possessed one, the sort of people who had yet to notice that both their laptop and mobile phone had calculators built into their software. She took on their messy lives and interesting jobs and ensured that, in one simple area, at least, they became orderly and predictable. It wasn't a career. It would lead her nowhere and meant nothing to her emotionally but it paid her bills and gave her the quiet satisfaction of knowing that, like a dry cleaner's or a baker's, her skills would always be needed.

This morning's client was a typical case, a fairly successful screenwriter and poet – not a friend – who, once a year, sent Laura a huge Jiffy bag into which she had stuffed twelve months of bank and credit-card statements, invoices, royalty statements and receipts for absolutely everything. Having sorted the large paperwork into calendar order, Laura proceeded to do the same with the receipts, smoothing them out, taking a magnifying glass and annotating pencil to the ones she couldn't immediately decipher and discarding any that were plainly never going to be offset against the client's tax bill.

She had a system involving twelve multicoloured wire post trays, one for each month, and a little notebook in which she meticulously noted the client's name and the time at which each bout of work on their behalf began and ended. She even had a stopwatch for work-related phone calls. Most of her clients worked from home and, nervous about capital gains tax, needed reassurance as to what percentage of domestic bills they could claim back and what proportion of their car and petrol expenses should count for work and what for private use. Some, like the piano tuner, the cello teacher and the graphic designers, drove a lot as part of their jobs; others, like the screenwriter/poet, hardly used their cars for work at all and made a great effort to post letters or buy stationery on every trip in the car so that the trip could at least partially count as work related.

The screenwriter/poet either lived in a huge house or appeared to have refurnished and decorated her study several times in as many years. She would probably have been appalled to know how closely Laura noted this expenditure and how far reaching were her powers of recall. In fact Laura couldn't have cared less so long as the numbers made sense and were recorded in the right places. The figures involved were relatively tiny and would be most unlikely ever to attract an inspector's attention. Nevertheless she felt it her duty to keep clients on their toes by asking perhaps two awkward questions a year about the hotel bill from Mauritius (research for a thriller involving a soured honeymoon, apparently) or the four-figure one from an Italian lighting designer (so tricky to find the reading lamp that really *works* for one) if only to be sure they had an explanation in place.

She often heard people say that doing their accounts or filing their tax returns brought on an attack of paranoia but for her it was merely a combination of paperwork and number shuffling and she had always found numbers as soothing as wind in long grass. It was the certainty of them, the known-ness, especially now, that was so welcome. Would her mother lose her mind but live for ever? How would they cope if ever they needed a hoist or a walk-in shower or if Laura's health failed her? Quite unanswerable. But fifty-five percent of some-one's annual motoring expenses or seventy-five percent of their total telephone costs was simply calculated and tidily delivered to its rightful little box. Only the playful balancing-out of quadratic equations would have soothed her more.

The danger, of course, was that the work – especially the sorting of papers – was so undemanding that it left part of her mind free to roam, usually her memory.

Ben wasn't her first boyfriend, or her first lover. But the moment they met, at a raucous student party she and two friends had gate-crashed, and he kissed her on a pile of coats in a candlelit bedroom, he made his predecessors seem provisional. They came from different backgrounds. He was a sporty public school medic, a few years her senior, she was one of a small, twitchy state school gang who had unexpectedly found themselves in a bastion of privilege. Being with him, however, felt irreducibly right.

They were a gang of three that had formed when they were assigned rooms on the same landing in their first year. Laura, who had only recently been able to make her U official, Tris, short for Tristram, who was gay and Mancunian and actually a secret Steve, and Amber, who was short and spiteful and had always been Amber.

Amber and Tris had found each other a few days earlier and badly needed a third to balance them out so Laura, who was in need of camouflage, had little choice in the matter. Tris was a chemist and Amber was reading English but the three of them became inseparable and went everywhere together. The only thing that threatened their uneasy camaraderie was other people in the shape of sex and so long as dirt was duly and promptly dished and the potential boyfriends reduced to *shags*, other people were no threat. In the messily exploratory way of students it was usually sex, not love. The group's relentless cross-questioning and commentary nipped any threat of love in the bud.

Unsmiling and sarcastic, Amber needed to be bad. She was highly sexed, available and eye-wateringly unfussy. She rarely slept with the same boy twice unless she could rest assured they were only coming back for more because they thought she was easy. She despised boyfriends and fidelity as bourgeois but tended to get weepy and aggressive if the subject of rape arose. She wheedled the *Dr Zhivago* story out of Laura (which Laura immediately regretted as it felt like handing her ammunition) and pointed out she had got off lightly since she could have been christened Tonya, after the character played by Geraldine Chaplin in the film, who didn't even get a theme.

Tris was far sunnier and thought of himself as romantic. He tended to fall only for boys who overlooked him or were too straight even to notice the way he was looking at them. When anyone did have the temerity to sleep with him, he despised them so vociferously afterwards Laura suspected he was actually rather hopeless in bed and just lay there like an ailing seal until it was over.

When Ben led her past them up the stairs of the ramshackle party house in Southmoor Road, she caught them watching with almost comical indignation and smiled at them. Nobody had ever led her by the hand before. She was still smiling when they knocked on her door in college the following afternoon, having lain in wait to watch for her eventual return, demanding tea and details. Tris was wounded because he had always wanted Ben for himself, claiming to have heard on good authority he was bisexual, but was placated by the news there was, at least, a camp younger brother. Amber sensed intuitively why Laura wasn't prepared to give details.

'Oh fuck,' she said. 'Tonya thinks he's special. Tris? Fig rolls, darling. Now. Was he all choked up and repressed? Did he swear when he came? That sort usually does, as if you've tricked them into lowering their guard. Christ, he didn't read you Rupert Brooke, did he? Stop *smiling*, Lazza, or I'll break something you love.'

But all Laura would say was that it was lovely. That *he* was lovely.

He was quite noisy in bed, in fact. He kept gasping and crying out.

'Shush!' she said at first. 'Quiet!' Beside herself with embarrassment at the thought that everyone on his staircase would hear. It was a bit over the top, but then she saw he really couldn't help it and that pleasure seized him and had to find a voice. He cried out into her hair and her pillow and she found it touching and felt thrillingly adult suddenly, both aroused and protective.

Her friends did their best to put her off him. Tris claimed to find him uptight and boring. Amber drew attention to little physical details like the way he sweated with nerves when she and Tris were quizzing him or the way he wore old-fashioned leather shoes, half-brogues in fact, when most of them were in pointy ankle boots or Converse trainers. This being long before mobile phones, they all used to keep sheets of paper pinned to their doors so that disappointed callers could leave messages. Laura took to hiding from the others – easily done since they were incapable of climbing her long staircase without chattering on the way – and the messages left on her sheet grew shorter and ever less amusing.

Laura was fairly sure Ben's friends were no more supportive than hers, although he was far too loyal to say so. She couldn't have been less like the privately educated girls his group favoured – girls with long, well-brushed hair, girls who wore dresses without irony, curiously unanimated girl-goddesses like Chloë Burstow who were unfailingly polite but exuded that supreme confidence born of knowing they knew how to behave in every situation, girls who saw nothing wrong with being called girls. His friends behaved towards her the way their mothers had taught them, boys giving up chairs and opening doors, girls tirelessly finding one thing she was wearing or carrying, however insignificant, they could praise. If she encountered them without Ben, however, accidentally sitting among them at dinner or breakfast, for instance, they were rude in the non-specific way of the well-brought-up.

None of this mattered. When she and Ben were alone together, they fitted and it felt so right it barely warranted discussion. They adjusted in no time to functioning as students with their brains fogged by sleep deprivation and sex. In the Christmas and then the Easter holidays they rented space in an acquaintance's Jericho house – that very house in Southmoor Road where the party had

thrown them together. There they played at everyday
domesticity, buying and cooking food together, sharing
a sofa to watch telly, going to bed early and actually
reading there: sweetly mundane activities from the non-
student world. Those were her clearest memories of their
time together – not their lovemaking, although they went
at that with all the abundant compulsiveness of youth,
but their playing house.

'Damn!' Her mother's voice. 'Ow!'

Laura looked up to find Mummy teetering by the
house door with a cup of coffee in either hand instead of
her walking frame. She was spilling one of the mugs and
had scalded her hand.

'Damn,' Laura echoed her, noting down the time in
her client book then slipping out of the shed. 'Sorry,' she
called. 'Lost all track of time. Here. Let me take those
then we can see to your hand. Lovely dress.'

'Yes. I like it.'

The scald wasn't serious as it was only reheated breakfast coffee and Mummy hadn't learnt how to use the
microwave properly. They drank what was left, leaning
in the kitchen, and munching the sort of luxurious, old
lady biscuits she would never have bought while Laura's
father was still alive, then Laura drove her to the hospital.

Mummy had an old, sun-bleached Austin Allegro,
once cherry red, now a sort of bird-spattered pink,
which Laura was insured to drive now that her own

driving days seemed to have passed. Mummy had modified her passenger seat with an old round leather cushion on top of a plastic carrier bag, which made it easier for her to swivel her inflexible legs in and out at either end of the journey. Now that walking any distance was beyond her, outings in the car, however routine or banal, took on the character of jaunts and were a source of excitement. Laura would force herself to drive slowly so her mother could notice things and comment on them.

The Falls Clinic was actually a thinly disguised research project. In exchange for submitting to various tests of reflex, cognition and short-term memory, patients – all of whom had suffered damaging falls in the past three years – were given a two-course lunch and were taught techniques for reaching for things they had dropped and put through exercises to improve their ability at righting themselves after a tumble and sometimes, to Mummy's disgust, to sharpen their mental focus.

Mummy disliked it because the nurses called her by her Christian name without asking and because the other patients tended to be too woolly in the head to provide much social stimulus. But she respected the value of scientific research and enjoyed the ping-pong – a game at which she had learnt to excel at Summerglades.

Laura treasured the precious three hours of solitude the clinic gave her but suspected she did not make the best use of them. Some of the patients were brought by ambulance or hospital car but a few were always dropped off by their carers and she couldn't help making comparisons. Did she look as worn already as that one or as thin lipped and humourless as that? She noted the way some were wildly overprotective of their charges and others almost off-hand. Apart from one younger sibling, who didn't look far off needing hip-protective pants herself, they were all, she guessed, dutiful children or children-in-law. It was heartening to imagine these people seizing the next three hours as an opportunity to embrace afresh activities set aside as no longer feasible – riding motorbikes, attending life classes, having daylight liaisons with other able-bodied persons – but she suspected that most would pass the time in a state of shocked vacancy, reading a newspaper perhaps or simply lying on their sofas staring at the ceiling, wondering where their lives and energy had gone. The saddest would spend the parentless interval *catching up* on housework and household shopping and so avoid dangerous introspection entirely.

She realized she had never found out which part of the hospital housed Ben's GUM clinic and was so busy scanning the signs around her that she drove off in a lurching rush, earning herself a glare from a woman battling to fit a walking frame into the rear of her hatchback without scratching new paintwork.

She chose to have a sandwich and fruit at her desk, for all the world as if she were working in a busy office, not her mother's garden shed. By picking-up time, she would have sorted the screenwriter/poet's paperwork, entered the figures in her computer and compiled several more awkward questions to ask her.

LUNCH BREAK

Periodically – it felt like once a month but was probably less – all GUM and HIV staff were expected to attend a drugs lunch in a seminar room in the hospital's main buildings. They had endured these at Ben's Chelsea and Westminster job too and the format was drearily familiar. A drugs company laid on a spread of sandwiches, fruit and chocolate bars in exchange for the chance to promote the virtues of new or infinitesimally improved products, to answer questions and to dole out samples and promotional freebies rarely more tempting than pens, notepads and the very occasional tee shirt. Both the GUM clinic and the HIV one were under constant pressure from the hospital's management to keep within budget and were obliged to seek best value for money at every turn so these grim little sessions were a necessary evil. Ben had learnt that the trick was to pile his plate with lunch, sit at the back, ask one question to ensure his presence had registered then sink into a state of restorative torpor such as he hadn't enjoyed since school divinity lessons.

Today he could neither relax as he would like nor concentrate for once on the drug reps' presentations. He ate his sandwiches and gulped his lukewarm apple juice but found he could not forget it was a Friday. Laura would be calling in to drop her mother off at the geriatric clinic.

Chloë always said he had a lousy memory, and he played along with her image of him as the absent-minded boffin who forgot his own birthday, because it suited him and marital acquiescence was easier than trying to change her opinion. Secretly he had always believed his memory was a useful mental sieve, sifting out the things that mattered – phone numbers, pin numbers, the Latin names of viruses and pseudo-Greek ones of drugs. His memory discarded dinner-party conversations even as they were unspooling around him, and he was ruthless, despite his best efforts, at refusing to store the names and even faces of people he didn't respect or simply hoped never to meet again. But he had always thought his ability to recollect events was better than average and liked to think he would make a useful eyewitness in a court case.

In the weeks after they rediscovered each other, Laura laid waste this idea he had of himself. With quiet ruthlessness, she brought him to see that what he thought of as the historical truth of their shared history was only a version, a narrative he had unconsciously shaped to cause the least pain for others and least blame for himself.

He did not recognize her immediately – twenty years had passed and they were in a hospital corridor, after all, not a reunion in college, so he was not looking for old faces. He emerged from a crowded lift and she was standing several yards away. She had caught something – a piece of gravel perhaps – in her shoe and was balancing on one foot while she lifted the other behind her and twisted around to free her heel of its irritation. He didn't normally notice clothes – not such a strong eyewitness after all, perhaps – but he remembered her sleeveless dress was simple and fairly short, the colour of a favourite pair of suede shoes Chloë had forcibly retired and not let him replace, a brown somewhere between bread crust and butterscotch. It was either very well cut or she had an excellent figure; without her inside it would surely have looked like a sack. Her arms and legs were lightly tanned and her short hair hung across her face as she arched backwards. She was anonymous and elegant, and elegance in a busy general hospital was as unexpected as dancing.

Then she stood upright again, glanced at her watch and looked about her, looking straight through him, with a hot, cross expression on her face, and he was sure it was her, even with the shorter, discreetly coloured hair. She took a step or two away from him then stopped and repeated the gesture because whatever was wrong in her shoe was still not right, and he looked again at her heel and flexing calf muscle and out of nowhere had a vivid recollection of how it felt when she pressed the sole of her foot into the much bigger sole of his as they lay end to end on a sofa and laughed and said, 'I can actually see you all the way round!'

He called her name, or said it tentatively, thinking that if it wasn't her he could walk on and pretend he was calling out to someone else. And she looked round. It was definitely her, but she still looked straight through him and he thought *twenty years* and remembered he was in a suit and getting his father's jowls and had greying hair. He was tempted to duck back into the crowd and walk swiftly in the opposite direction.

When she did recognize him it was such a relief he asked her out before he had gathered his wits sufficiently to be nervous. She glanced at his wedding ring, much as he did with patients, but she said yes, in a day or two, and they took out their mobiles to exchange numbers.

They never went on dates as students; they were too poor. Like all their peers they went about things in the reverse order to the practice of their parents' generation. They had sex, realized they got on really well then fell in love. His recollection was that the love part in their case had been naïve and simple, consisting largely of saying *I do love you* a lot, usually when in bed, and hardly carried over at all into their daily lives as students. She continued to see her friends, he his, and the two groups had no common ground. He remembered the relationship as existing within a kind of bubble. He remembered no great trauma at its ending, simply a kind of regretful, muted cadence as the relentlessly realistic demands of medicine took over. Compared to his courtship of Chloë, whom he only took up with after finals, it was a delicate, dreamlike affair conducted largely at night.

Chloë was all for the bright pragmatism of day and in many ways, looking back, it was she who courted him. She shyly got a mutual friend – a school friend who hated one of Laura's friends for some reason – to introduce them as she confessed to having a spare ticket to their college's ball. She took him to meet her parents – the bullying, newly titled surgeon and his polite, browbeaten shadow of a wife – and he remembered wondering if Chloë were programmed to marry medicine. Then the physical infatuation he felt with her, the disgracefully blokeish pleasure and pride her proximity aroused in him, was reinforced by the potent persuasion of suddenly feeling his life joined up. His friends knew her friends and both sides heartily approved the match. And it *was* a match, in their eyes, whereas the other, the thing with Laura, his mates had treated as odd, dirty fun, as if he'd had a girlfriend who wasn't even a student ...

All of which made them sound hateful but they weren't. They were lovely, decent people. They cared. But far more than he, the anomalous scholarship cuckoo in their midst, they were products of careful upbringing, insistently trained to conform, or only to rebel within carefully circumscribed parameters, and inculcated with a deep sense of insecurity when away from their own kind.

He had thought of none of this for years, twenty years, until he took Laura on a date to a restaurant where, characteristically, she insisted in advance she would be paying her share in a way that Chloë, despite a hefty trust fund, never had.

They had exchanged numbers and made a vague agreement to go out once she had had time to settle her mother back home and time to settle in herself, but he could have avoided ringing her and ignored her call if she rang him. They had run into each other just when he was especially depressed about his marriage, however, just beginning to admit to himself that it had been a mistake, so it seemed like a piece of fate. He had retained few close friends and they were all married, child-bearingly and happily so, apparently, and to voice doubts about a marriage to anyone in such a tight-knit group of people was to unstopper a baleful genie. Laura stood in isolation from the rest of his life and always had. And exes, even exes not seen in twenty years, surely knew one and understood one in ways friends never could. It was only supper, he told himself, an innocent, catch-up supper. If he told her about him and Chloë it would go no further and anyone, even Chloë, would understand friends who hadn't seen each other in twenty years wanting to catch up.

Laura was a friend. That was his overwhelming sense in the redfaced minutes after running into her in the hospital – not that she was a former girlfriend but that she was a long-lost boon companion. Nonetheless, when Chloë rang on the afternoon of their supper and left a message – some mundane query about service charges in their block of flats – he texted her back an answer rather than risk ringing her, for fear that he might blurt out with whom he was about to spend the evening.

Luckily the restaurant was not too quiet. It was on the raised ground floor of a handsome Georgian house in a row of such houses near the county court, most of which were given over to barristers' chambers and estate agents. The atmosphere was clubbily masculine and unfussy – with dark wood, white linen, candlelight and pretty young waitresses who sounded as though their fathers might eat there. He ordered calf's liver, she a rare steak without the chips and, since neither of them was driving, they shared a bottle of claret. Then their waitress left them alone to talk and the twenty-year gap came home to him afresh.

They were edgily polite at first, re-establishing that Laura had moved there from Paris to care for her mother, he from London to care for his brother, then she had seemed to challenge him.

'So you went and married Chloë Burstow,' she said.

'Yes,' he said and heard himself apologize.

'Are you?' she asked. 'Sorry, I mean?'

'Of course. I … I …' He fell silent.

She topped up his wine. 'She always scared me, you know.'

'No! Who? Chloë?'

'Yes. She was so composed, so grown up. We all wanted to hate her, of course, because she was rich and did modelling. So we used to bitch and say how she was so reserved because she was actually very thick. People claimed she'd failed Oxbridge but then somehow been found miraculously to have passed it after all once Daddy made a donation to the college.'

'Mummy. It's her mother that had the money. She married down but, because he got a handle for services to medicine, people didn't always realize.'

'*Ah, bon?*'

'And Chloë isn't stupid, not at all. She's just not …' He shuffled his wineglass.

'Clever,' Laura supplied.

'No,' he admitted then glanced up. 'You're laughing at me, aren't you?'

'I'm in deadly earnest.'

'It's odd,' he said. 'I can't think clearly when I'm near her. My only power in the marriage comes when we're apart. She may not be a brain surgeon but there's a persuasive strength to her that …' He broke off, seeing Laura was frowning. 'Sorry. This is the last thing you want to talk about.'

'Nonsense. It's your last twenty years. What else are we going to talk about?'

Then she smiled with a bracing kind of solicitude and he knew he could tell her anything. 'I think the marriage is probably over,' he admitted. He had told nobody this until then. 'We're not divorced or anything. But having to move here for a bit because of Bobby and being without her has made me see things more clearly. It's only a question of time and courage. We never loved each other. Not really. I think we both see that now.'

'Honestly?' she asked.

'No,' he admitted slowly, as much to himself as her. 'I think she probably loves me. In some awful way I think she loves me more as she senses me withdrawing from her. Her father's such a bastard I benefit by comparison without even trying. She sort of needs me to balance him. She thinks I'm good. The Good Doctor.'

'And aren't you?'

'I'm just a doctor who hasn't put money first. That hardly makes me a saint. But she … We haven't spoken properly, not honestly, for ages. She forwards my mail and sometimes scribbles cross little notes on the back of it.'

'Doesn't she ring you?'

He sighed.

She smiled wistfully. 'Oh dear. Of course she rings. Are there children?'

'No, thank God. But that's one of the things that made me realize about us. She wants them desperately. We can't seem to have them and although she's quite prepared to adopt I realized I wasn't because I didn't want to have children with her. I suddenly knew I couldn't make that commitment. And then Mum dying and Bobby going to pieces gave me the perfect escape route. Isn't that pathetic?'

'No,' she said. 'A bit male but not pathetic. Poor her, though.'

'Not really. Well. Okay. Poor her.'

And as if by mutual consent, Chloë was not mentioned between them again all evening.

She wasn't quite the Laura he remembered, but then both their younger selves had been keeping things back, posing even, in their eagerness to make, then sustain, an impression. She was still solemn and funny, still keener to make him talk than to reveal much herself, but something since they had parted, Paris perhaps, other men more than possibly, had led her to develop, what? An edge? That sounded unpleasant and it wasn't that. A strength, then, he did not remember. It suited her, like her quiet, carefully chosen clothes and shorter hair, whose colour she dismissed, when he admired it, as *enhanced mouse*.

'Why Paris?' he asked.

'I was terribly unhappy.' She tore open the bread roll she had carefully chosen when they were offered, but didn't eat it. She sipped her wine then saw he was waiting for more. 'No,' she said. 'That sounds too dramatic and it wasn't. Not a breakdown or anything. But I'd lost my way and made some stupid mistakes and had a really stupid, damaging relationship I never should have had.

It gave me a fresh start of sorts. It was a sort of rather overdue finishing school.' She smiled at herself then up at him. 'Then it became a habit. You never said you had a brother who needed looking after. You only ever said he was a bit camp.'

'You know how students are. Reinventing themselves. Grabbing the chance to be defined on their own terms for once. You never said your parents were naturists.'

'Can you blame me? It was bad enough they were academics and sent me to a state school. I'd never have heard the end of it. I'd have been a pariah.'

'You? Never.' But he remembered his judgemental friends and mutely agreed with her.

'Yes I would. My friends were the rebels, remember.'

'That dreadful tramp with the hair. Ruby.'

'Amber.' She laughed softly to herself. 'Whatever became of her? City, probably. A real ball-buster in a Prada suit.'

'And that skinny boy.'

'Tristram? Poor Tris. It was when everyone, even straight boys, was trying to be Sebastian Flyte and he looked like the Emcee from *Cabaret*. Completely unwholesome.'

'He used to unnerve me because I'd hear him chattering away in your room as I came up those stairs and the second I came in he'd go silent and watchful. I never got a word out of him. And she made me so nervous.'

'Tris fancied the pants off you.'

'He *didn't*. He just thought I was prematurely middle-aged and uncool.'

'Well, yes. But he still had gangbang fantasies about you and your Wykehamist hearties. You know the things state school poofs dream about boarding school ...'

'Lies. All of it.'

'Yeah. Right.'

'So what became of him? You said *poor Tris*.'

'Oh. The expected.'

Their waitress approached with food and Laura's gravity vanished as she smiled up at her and said thanks.

'He was one of the earliest ones,' she went on once they were alone again. 'Died, what, two years after we'd ... I think he was much wilder than he ever let on to Amber.'

'He probably died on my ward. God.'

'Really?'

'Back then there wasn't a wide range of places to send people.'

Blood ran out of her steak as she sliced it open, which she casually mopped up with a piece of bread. He must have been looking disconcerted because she caught his eye and said, 'Sorry. What can I say? Paris.'

Later on, when their coffee arrived, they sat back a little, watching each other while the waitress cleared detritus off their table. She smiled to herself once they were alone again.

'The next bit's much easier in French,' she said.

'What would happen in French?' he asked.

'Oh, something eloquent and brief, like a shrug or an *et alors*.'

He stirred in sugar he never normally took, because her sudden direct glance had made him nervous. 'Et alors,' he said in his best schoolboy accent and he felt her toe brush his calf.

'Thought you'd never ask,' she said.

Where to go was a problem. Her mother was a light sleeper apparently and he was anxious not to unsettle Bobby having not long found him a job and established a steady domestic routine with him. It was Laura who gently pointed out that the restaurant was part of a hotel, much used by visiting lawyers and unlikely to blanch at an impromptu booking.

He was jaded by years of marriage but suspected their first bedroom reunion was a disaster. He was far too eager and they were both freshly conscious of how their bodies had aged in twenty years. He was no longer a sportsman.

'Do you mind?' she asked, reaching for the bedside light switch and he said,

'Not at all,' and was frankly relieved but then he tripped on her discarded shoes and they managed to bump noses quite painfully and one of numerous pillows sent her glass of water flying, which gave the bed an untimely wet patch.

But when they were finished, passion clumsily spent, and able simply to lie there, an amazing calm came over him, a certainty and sense of rightness, as though his

PATRICK GALE

whole being had sighed *at long bloody last*. He held her close, breathed the scent in her hair and thought, *enhanced mouse*.

'What?' she murmured.

'I didn't say anything.'

'You laughed at something.'

'I feel as though I just came home,' he said. 'That's all. Oh God.'

'Oh,' she said. 'That.' And she turned the lamp back on and discovered it had a built-in dimmer so they lay for what felt like hours but was only about forty minutes, talking quietly, patching up torn years, until Laura, who had been conscientiously clock watching, sighed and slipped away from him and into the shower.

So it started.

In the weeks that followed they returned several times to the hotel because it was a treat and felt like a space outside time, unlike their respective lodgings. But it was expensive and evenings could be difficult as her mother and Bobby were home and needed feeding. Urgency helped them overcome their fear of daylight and they took to snatching time together during Ben's lunch hour, when Bobby was safely at work. They usually hurried to his house where they drew ineffective curtains and defied the thinness of the walls but on Fridays her mother attended the Falls Clinic for three hours and Laura would drive him back down St James Lane for a precious forty-five minutes in the middle, to the little, feminine Eden she shared with the old woman.

He was tantalized by the glimpses he got of her mother about the place as Laura hurried him through the house to her room, especially from the journals piled by her chair, and would have liked to meet her, not least because she was a virologist and he had never quite lost his boyhood fascination with her subject. But he was reminded soon after meeting Laura again of her ingrained habit of secrecy and way of keeping people in discrete compartments. As a student she had dismissed any enquiries about her parents – 'He's a bearded sociologist, she studies viruses. Blah. Not interesting.' – with a vigour that made him wonder if she did not struggle to emerge from their shadow. In this respect she had changed little as an adult and, although he had never suffered from overbearing parents, Chloë and her father had taught him to respect a person's desire to be judged on their own merit, accepted as an individual, not as a mere adjunct to a family.

'Time enough,' he thought. 'We can meet when she's ready.'

By degrees she let slip or he wrung out of her the shaming truth about their past; that the apparent aplomb with which she accepted their split as students had been youthful bravado. In fact she had gone to pieces, in her restrained way, and found herself unable to sit her finals.

She clearly hadn't meant to tell him but he stupidly blundered on with quizzing her about why she had never pursued her career in maths, or not in the expected way, given the degree she was taking and how well she had been doing, and finally she said,

'Because I never sat the bloody degree, okay? I pretended. Amber and Tris thought I was sitting my papers. I came to breakfast in my silly subfusc like everyone else, even got sick with nerves, but then I just walked around or sat in cafés and the cinema. I went to one paper and it was so hideous just sitting there writing nothing that I couldn't stand any more.'

'But surely you could have told someone? Got counselling?'

'It wasn't like that back then. Don't you remember anything? Even kids who pretended to be sick or mad had to sit their papers in hospital.'

She was right. He remembered then the chilling old myth of the student who in desperation tipped boiling water over his hands to avoid having to sit a philosophy paper, being compelled to dictate his essays instead.

'You should have told me,' he said.

'Don't be stupid,' she said. 'You were running after Chloë by then, doing a Brideshead. I might have been going to pieces but I had my pride.'

They were in his bed at the time, in the half-light shed through unlined curtains. They had not long made love and their mingling warmth and scents and the touch of her hand through his hair softened by a few degrees the sudden harshness of her tone, but he found he could not answer her. And his silence, followed a minute later by her abrupt departure, with her clothes, for the bathroom, felt like their first row.

And then, just a week ago, the stupidest thing happened. It was his birthday and, yes, he had completely forgotten. It was a Friday, Falls Clinic day, and Laura was going to collect him from the hospital at lunchtime. But, at the end of his morning clinic, Chloë showed up, out of the blue, with a ridiculously exquisite birthday cake from the Southwark pâtisserie she favoured. He emerged from writing-up his final patient of the morning and there she was, sitting in the men's waiting room, chatting affably with one of the camper nurses. (Gay men loved Chloë, effortlessly undone and enslaved by her combination of beauty and apparent vulnerability.)

Coming upon her without warning in that setting, amongst the free condom baskets and the chlamydia pamphlets, would have been startling at any time but it was doubly so when he had spent the morning only half-listening to patients as he thought about what Laura had told him and how he must tell Chloë all, cease this wounding ambiguity and make a clean break with her. And suddenly there she was, the cruelly peremptory answer to an unspoken wish, and his resolve left him at the sight of her. She looked particularly smart and groomed, as though for lunch with girlfriends, and brave, as though calling in like this had taken courage. They kissed, he thanked her for the cake, which they both knew would be wolfed by the nurses that afternoon, and steered her away from the clinic and up the hill towards her car.

'I know you're busy. I know you're working,' she said. 'I just didn't want you to think I'd forgotten.' She didn't make demands or a scene or deliver an ultimatum or a solicitor's letter. She didn't even want to stay for lunch. Possibly she was on her way to visiting someone else – she was a mistress of barely conscious multi-tasking and had a way of judiciously measuring out appointments in advance. But it was a lovely gesture, a sweet one by her lights, given how tense their last parting had been. Her timing couldn't have been worse, however, because, as he walked her back to her car, apologizing for being so hopeless and uncommunicative and beginning to suggest it was time they talked things through but that a snatched lunch hour was not the moment, he saw Laura watching them from a sunny bench by the main building's back entrance.

'I know,' Chloë sighed. 'You're right. Don't apologize. I've been hopeless too. I'm such a coward. Bye, Ben. Happy birthday.' She reached up with the hand that was already holding her car keys and brought his head down to hers.

Thinking she was going to kiss him on the lips, aware, from the glimpse he had over her shoulder, of Laura walking smartly back to her mother's car, he half-flinched and she was obliged to press her lips quickly to his forehead in a clumsy kind of blessing.

As soon as she sped off, he turned towards Laura, but she drove off too without looking at him.

'Wait!' he shouted. 'Laura!'

He wouldn't have caught her, only she was held up by a traffic snarl at the exit and had to wind down her window when he ran up and tapped on it, panting.

'I've done this,' she told him, and held a palm up when he started to speak. 'No. Sorry, Ben. I've been a bit on the side. Been one for years. I could write the handbook. But I was never *your* mistress. You were always different, better, for all your faults, and I'd rather keep it that way. Sorry.' And she drove off.

He knew her mobile number. He gave her time to reach home then rang it. But she must have seen his name flash up and pressed ignore. Whenever he tried ringing her, as the afternoon clinic dragged on, it was the same. He tried texting her but got no further than *Please, Laura* before deleting his message unsent. He wrote her three letters over the Saturday, thinking he could drop off a letter by hand under cover of darkness, but he posted none of them. Her quiet hurt had cut to the quick of him as Chloë's sarcasm and accusations had never done.

Finally, on the Sunday afternoon, he could bear it no longer and decided simply to call round, face humiliation or rejection, anything to have the opportunity of seeing her again.

Perhaps because they had always been in such a hurry to reach her bed he had not noticed before how securely

107

the little house was enclosed. From some way down the hill one could glimpse the upper windows' white-painted Gothic frames but nothing could be seen from closer to but flinty wall and an impenetrable thicket of hedge shrubs topped by a lush tangle of roses. There was a gate in the wall, a door in effect, tall and firmly bolted. Cautiously, thinking it might be purely a decorative antique, he pulled a brass knob and was startled to find he had set a bell jangling fairly close to.

'Bugger!' said an old woman's voice from somewhere nearby then called out imperiously, 'Are you expecting anyone?' The distant answer was too faint for him to make out. 'Me neither,' said the voice. 'Oh well.'

What sounded like a shed door was opened then shut and then, abruptly, a little door half-opened behind a grille in the gate's middle and the old woman's voice asked if she could help him.

'I hope so,' he said. 'I've come to see Laura, if she's in. I'm Ben Patterson, an old Oxford friend of hers.'

'Well, how lovely. She didn't say. You must have tea.'

She slammed the little window closed again and opened the gate to admit him. She had on a faded but still elegant garment – a housecoat? Surely not a dressing gown? He assumed she was quite naked underneath but her manner, and years of practice, meant that one had no idea. She wore Dr Scholl sandals whose wooden heels clacked against the brick path as she shuffled ahead of him, leaning on her walker. 'My legs don't work any more,' she called over her shoulder. 'So dull. Laura? Your friend Ben has come for tea. Isn't that nice?'

'I don't remember you,' she went on as Laura called out a pale-faced *hi* from the front door which made him feel at once that he had broken an unspoken rule by barging in, 'but then it was a long time ago and Laura always enjoyed her secrets. Or not secrets exactly but keeping us all in separate compartments. Even her father and me she told quite different things.'

But Ben remembered her. He thought he was mistaken at first. There were a lot of highly educated women of her generation with a similarly distinguished manner; an air of high confidence and what their mothers would have thought an unfeminine directness of conversation born of making their way against considerable opposition in a largely masculine field. One met such women in any senior common room and on many a hospital board. So he might have been mistaken.

Laura emerged into the garden with a tray of tea things and cake and greeted him with a quick hug, as cool as a spy, betraying no trace of what had recently passed between them. She went through the motions of catching up, asking what had brought him to Winchester, offering her condolences on his mother's death, asking with concern how his brother was coping. Before carrying the teapot inside to refill it she explained to her mother that Ben was a venereologist and to Ben that virology had always been her mother's specialism.

'I thought I knew you,' he said. 'It's Professor Jellicoe, isn't it?'

'That's right. But I'm sorry I …'

'I'd never realized – with you having a different surname to Laura. I mean, I knew her mother was a virologist but I didn't know she was you. If you see what I mean. Oh, there's no reason why you should remember me,' he heard himself blathering on. 'It was a long time ago.' And, as Laura began to walk back from the house, he diverted Professor Jellicoe, lest she think him quite unhinged, with a question about the latest research into a link between herpes simplex and Alzheimer's. But he was reeling and took his leave soon after his third cup and second slice of cake.

He had thought what? That Laura had only to see him in the gateway to relent? That she would snatch a moment's conference with him to unsay hasty words, to arrange another date? Instead she mutely encouraged her mother to join her in waving him off so that they weren't left alone for one instant. The folly and egotism of his little visit weighed hard on him in the night which followed. But not quite so hard as the cowardly memories it had finally dragged out from the shadows.

Of course the old woman didn't remember him. He meant nothing to her. He was just another of the countless students she encountered every week, not faceless exactly but interchangeable in the way the young became as one aged. (Ben had the same problem already with medical students and student nurses – names and faces no sooner imprinted on his consciousness than a fresh batch took their place.)

It had been his last term, with the medical finals only days from starting and, as very occasionally happened, a group of particularly promising students was invited for Sunday lunch in the warden's lodgings. He remembered he had resented his own invitation deeply because he had detailed revision plans which accounted for every spare hour or two and the hours swallowed by sherry and lunch and coffee and polite chat afterwards would necessitate rearranging his timetable or covering some topic in less detail than he had intended.

Sulkily told of how he had been singled out, Laura had shrugged, deep in her own revision of Graph Theory, and advised him simply to ignore the invitation or say no as he had more important things on his mind than being nice to old fogeys. But he knew it wasn't done to say no and a school friend, the one who disliked Amber so because she laughed out loud when he made a pass at her – he remembered that detail now – impressed on him that, being a scientist, the warden often had senior research fellows or surgeons among his guests, the very people who might be considering Ben's applications in the months to come.

So he ironed a shirt, nailbrushed the worst of the food stains off his only suit and joined the small clutch of undergraduates huddling outside the warden's lodgings at twelve-thirty. The warden's wife astutely pressed them

111

all to circulate and interact with the all-important grown-ups rather than mooch in corners with one another.

Ben hadn't thought of this for years. Now he distinctly remembered, however, how he had been charged with a huge plate of chicken satay on sticks, which was still such unfamiliar fare then that the warden's wife impressed on him he was to warn people it contained peanuts and was quite spicy.

They were entertained in a beautiful first-floor room overlooking the warden's private garden. The Georgian portraits, highly polished floor, old silk rugs and pillowy sofas conveyed an air of adult privilege that was as intoxicating as the unaccustomed midday sherry. He soon found he had forgotten all about revision, or at least forgotten to worry about it, and was enjoying himself. He fell into conversation with an affable, bow tied art historian from the Courtauld whose erudition and worldliness would have been intimidating had Ben been sober. With something alarmingly like flirtation, he ordered Ben not to move because the satay was so preferable to the slightly slimy vol-au-vents on offer. He introduced Ben to the portraits, explaining, in terms Ben failed to remember, why Ramsay was so much more interesting than Gainsborough.

'But painting's not really your thing, is it?' he asked, wolfing another piece of chicken and waving to the warden's wife in a way that kept her at bay.

'Not really,' Ben said. 'I mean, I look and sometimes I like but …'

'Yes, quite. *But.* What does interest you?'

Ben thought of the revision he was skipping to be getting rapidly drunk in that beautiful room and started to talk about syphilis.

'In which case you must meet The Jellicoe.'

'Who?'

'Harriet!'

A woman who had only just come in and seemed happy to be claimed kissed him briefly then was introduced to Ben as Professor Jellicoe, Virus Queen.

'Really, Howard,' she protested, but the art man had abandoned them in search of fresh prey. ' Sorry,' she said. 'Is virology your thing too or had you just bored him?' When Ben explained that it was and that it was what he should at that moment have been revising, she said that was easily remedied as he could sit by her and have a sort of tutorial. 'You'll be doing me a favour,' she said, 'as I was dreading this and I have no small talk. What have you read recently?'

He mentioned a year-old article on Marburg Virus and she countered it with two other suggestions including a great tome called simply *Filoviridae* he couldn't possibly read in the time left before the exam but whose thesis she would do her best to summarize for him.

When they proceeded into the dining room she brazenly evicted the Eng Lit student placed beside her in favour of Ben. 'Well, I'd be no use to *her,*' she said. As soon as they sat, she politely but irrefutably informed the student on her left, who in any case was a physicist, so

113

of little interest to her, that she and her other neighbour had *much to discuss*. For the next ninety minutes she grilled Ben and drilled him, suggesting which topics he should concentrate on and which lines of argument would play best with the doctors she suspected were marking his papers. And she scribbled a bullet point summary of the *Filoviridae* argument on an old airmail envelope she produced from her bag.

'Thank you so much,' he stammered, when it was announced that coffee would be served in the room where they had first assembled. 'I just wish I could have taken notes while you were talking.'

'Waste of time,' she said. 'What you don't remember without notes will be of no use to you in an exam in four days' time. It's been a pleasure talking to you. You're hoping for a first, naturally.'

'Well ...'

'The college is, of course. That's why you're here.'

He thought of Laura, who passionately wished for a first in maths to please her parents, but had not been invited to one of these lunches, and felt treachery, then guilt, then an unexpected and sickening slippage in his feelings towards her.

'Consider my research programme at Imperial when making your applications.'

'I will. Of course I will,' he gushed. 'Thank you.'

'Have you got a girlfriend or something?' she asked bluntly. Almost everyone had left or was leaving the table and they were virtually alone there.

'Er. Well, yes,' he said. 'We've been going out for two terms now.'

'But nothing serious? You're not engaged or anything?'

'No,' he admitted, perplexed.

'Good,' she exclaimed, gently slapping the table edge beside her. 'You'll think me old-fashioned but there's nothing more depressing than students just embarking on important research who go and get married. Such a mistake. Such a drain. Either they drop out, because they suddenly need to make money, or they simply lose their focus and I end up having to dump them. If she's really keen, let her down gently but let her down all the same. At least for the next few years. Your work *has* to come first. I never married exactly but I *settled* very young – I thought it was just part of being adult – something one had to do – and it was such a mistake.' She thumped the table again.

'You're not together any more?'

'Yes. Still together and happily so but –' She touched his forearm and her grasp was like steel as she looked so deeply into his face that he could smell the wine on her breath and see a stray eyelash that had caught on her cheek. 'Love is an amazing thing but – there's no nice way to put this that won't sound arrogant but what the hell – for exceptional people, for people like you, it's nearly always *diminishing*.'

Something in the way she said that word chilled him and, as she stood to obey the repeated summons of the

115

warden's wife to come and admire something rare that was flowering for the first time in the garden and bade him a curt goodbye, Ben stood too and found he was shivering. It wasn't cold or fear at work but a kind of excitement, as at something momentous that had to be done but would require courage and a stern, monastic steadfastness.

He broke up with Laura that afternoon. If she had wept or raged at him or even argued he wouldn't have gone through with it. He assumed she would argue, half-hoped it, and that she'd convince him to change his mind. He heard again now with chilling clarity his pompous, cack-handed explanation that he wasn't ready to get serious, that he couldn't afford to commit to anyone because of the need to focus on his further studies.

All she asked was, 'Is there someone else?' to which he quite honestly – for it was true at the time – answered no. 'So it's me, then?' she asked to which he said,

'No. Of course not. It's me. It's all me.' Which, he now reflected bitterly, was also true and had continued to be the case. All the mess began and ended with him and his egotistic dithering and need for approval.

As he left her rooms and hurried down the long staircase that led back to Holywell Quad, he had started to shudder with adrenalin again. He had felt sorrow, of course he did, but also a self-dramatizing thrill at the enormity of the sacrifice he had just made. He might never meet anyone as lovely again. He might be doomed to become one of the boffin bachelors the students laughed at, the sort with odd socks or egg stains on his tie. But it would be in a noble cause; he would have dedicated himself like a monk or, more alluringly, some kind of chaste knight.

He sought out his school friends, who shared a set of rooms overlooking the garden, and told them at once, so as to make it real and stop himself wavering. Once again he half-hoped for a stay of execution, that these naysayers would suddenly change their tune, tell him he was mad and she was one in a million and that he must run back to her at once and beg.

They were startled but they were also relieved and only now told him in full all the reservations they'd entertained about Laura but had only hinted at before, about her suitability for him. This denigration of her pained him but he couldn't explain why he had split up with her without sounding grotesquely ambitious and it was easier to let them make assumptions than have them tease him. They saw he was suffering and had the decency to change the subject but he was astonished at how easily destroyer had come to be treated as victim and every consideration shown him in the hours that followed was another splinter in his soul.

The fault was his not hers, as he had told her, and if he made himself break off from his furious revision to think of her, all that came to mind was the sad pallor of her face as she'd watched his windbaggy self-justification.

It was only after his exams were done and once his friends introduced him to Chloë and she had treated him to the college ball that he began to convince himself there *had* been something wrong about Laura, even as Chloë fulfilled Professor Jellicoe's gypsy warning to the letter by joining her father in pressuring him to pursue a clinical rather than a research route.

Chloë was demure, sexually a little shy, or at least she expertly conveyed that impression in their first weeks together. By comparison the almost sexless casualness with which Laura would drop her clothes and her honest eagerness to fall into bed came to seem odd, unfeminine, even slightly unhinged.

Chloë and Laura didn't know one another except as names and faces but colleges were small enough and Chloë was jealous enough that she found out about Laura with time and grilled girlfriends who had known her even slightly so that whenever the question of Ben's past love arose she would talk disparagingly about 'your North London hippie with the slutty friends' and established an official version of Laura as a muddy-soled bad girl and anarchist. It couldn't have been further from the truth but it flattered her by comparison and flattered him too, as though he had been somehow tamed but retained the capacity to run a little wild.

He emerged from his guilty reverie to find himself staring at the seminar room clock and suddenly knew that all that mattered to him would be waiting in the disabled parking spaces down below. Tolerance stretched to its limit, he stood in such a hurry the plastic beaker that had held his juice clattered off his table to the floor. 'Sorry,' he muttered as colleagues and drug reps looked round. 'Sorry. I've just got to er ...' And he slipped out. He'd plead a migraine, a stomach ache.

The lift stopped at an intervening floor, then at another. He cursed and pushed through a swing door onto the stairs and ran down them, dodging slowcoaches and apologizing to startled faces he encountered as he lurched around each twist in the stairwell.

The disabled parking bays Laura favoured were tucked into an unpromising side alley, the kind of lost courtyard that endlessly extended and adapted hospitals must have created the world over, which only the initiated would have any hope of finding. He sprinted out into the internal service road that led to it. Then he froze, panting ludicrously, and quickly backed into a doorway before she could spot him.

He had barely had time to see her reversing the old Austin out of its space and only now remembered that it was the time when she was collecting her mother rather than dropping her off. Of course she wasn't alone and of course he couldn't jump out into her path when Professor Jellicoe was there, beadily intelligent beside her.

As they passed him he dared to edge out to watch them go. The car was entirely uninteresting, old without character, an old lady's once-red automatic, undramatically scraped and dented from some negligent reversing.

Taking in its departing rear view then becoming aware of his sweaty shirtfront and racing heart, he felt deeply the absurd pass to which he had brought himself.

AFTERNOON NAP

❦

Because of the lingering smell of an institutional lunch –
fish pie, today, and pineapple sponge with custard – and
the early afternoon collecting time, the Falls Clinic had
more than ever the air of a geriatric kindergarten. Had
the patients emerged proudly clutching paintings on
sugar paper or spaceships made from egg boxes and
yoghurt pots instead of letters for their GPs, the illusion
would have been complete. Today they had even endured
story time in the shape of a cheery chat from a health
visitor about the importance of keeping well hydrated
whatever the continence challenges.

'A patronizing ninny,' Mummy pronounced. 'With
one of those bottle-top degrees.'

'Now how can you know that?'

'I asked her.'

'Mummy!'

'Well, I'd nothing to lose. I shan't be going back.'

'Why not?'

'They've finished with me, apparently. I've had my *allocation of clinic hours* and presumably they've gathered all the data they can get from me. Sorry,' she added. 'Tough on you.'

Laura attempted protest but it came out feebly and Mummy ignored it.

'I suppose I should sign up for classes. Architectural history, maybe, or a language. But they tend to happen in the evening and I'm so bloody sleepy then.'

'Why ever should you?'

'Oh. You know. Get out of your hair for a while.'

'It's your house. I should be getting out of yours.'

'Quite right, girl,' Mummy said rather sharply. 'Have an affair or something. Sorry. Filthy mood. It's the ninny's fault with her MA in Medical Humanities and Dance. I'll be better for a nap. Sorry.'

Back at the house, Mummy retreated to the downstairs lavatory while Laura put the car away then ushered her onto the tiny stair-lift that had only been installed with difficulty – the stairs were far narrower than the modern average – and helped her onto her bed. She took off her shoes and drew the curtains for her. She could tell Mummy was tired because she made no attempt to take off that day's going-out frock.

Laura knew she should make a start on the next client's figures but the afternoon light slanting across her own bedroom was too alluring and she kicked off her shoes and lay down too as Mummy's deep breathing from next door edged into regular, wistful snores.

She wouldn't sleep – she held out against the temptation of afternoon naps even when living in Paris – but she would let herself lie down for a few minutes, fully clothed, on top of the bedding. She listened to the snores, the birdsong, the electronic chirrup of a distant lorry's reversing signal and stared at the still unfamiliar furniture and pictures in her room. Pretty watercolours in battered gilt frames, a chest of drawers with a dressing table mirror on it topped by a little bird and some carved ribbon and a wardrobe, all in dark, richly polished wood. And a Globe-Wernicke bookcase.

Along with the summerhouse table, these bookcases, now scattered around the house, were the only objects Laura remembered from her childhood that her mother had retained. Heavier and more practical than the Georgian furniture, with glass doors that folded ingeniously over the tops of each row of books (as a child she called them *book garages*), they were incongruous and didn't really 'go' but her mother had always appreciated their way of keeping books free of dust.

The rest of it – pictures, tables, chairs, even beds – had belonged to Laura's maternal grandparents. She knew nothing about antiques, having grown up in a house where all furniture apart from the book garages was either built by her father or bought at Habitat.

Her father was a war orphan and her mother had broken off with (or been cast out by – the story varied) her family when she moved in with him. It was only all these years later, in her forties, that Laura saw the emotional significance of the modern furnishings with which she grew up. From what she could gather, Dad and Mummy came of violently different stock. His parents had run a political bookshop in Camden – bombed with his already war-widowed mother in its basement. He was not-quite-adopted for two years by the schoolmaster's family in Bournemouth who had taken him in as an evacuee, who ensured that he stuck with grammar school and made it through to the London School of Economics where he studied political science. Which was where, at some sort of political debate, he met Mummy.

She came of hunting Hampshire squirearchy and had bucked family tradition by not only having a brain but insisting on nurturing it. She had bullied her parents into semi-submission by claiming she was going to learn to treat horses at the Royal Veterinary College but had tricked them and jumped courses to study biology at Imperial, with every intention of specializing in viruses. She had been obsessed with these since a missionary had visited St Swithun's to lecture on leprosy.

She wasn't an only child – there was a brother farming in New Zealand and one who had stayed in Hampshire but showed an alarming preference for antiques and old women to marriage and horseflesh – but she was the only daughter and the protected youngest and her parents were disgusted when she not only took up with a bearded, rootless left-winger, and sociologist to boot, but moved in with him. She proved immune to both emotional blackmail and financial disinheritance and severed all ties with them as soon as they threatened to with her.

She had no great desire for motherhood and was living with a man who convinced her that the family was a patriarchal evil at the root of most of the modern world's ills, from poverty to depression, and she used multiple contraceptive methods, on the belt and braces principle. By the time Laura startled the household with her arrival, Mummy was a professor at Imperial College and a then fairly elderly thirty-five and Dad was a lecturer at South Bank Poly. They were a radical couple so set in their domestic ways it always surprised people to learn they weren't married.

Laura had an odd childhood. It wasn't an unhappy one – she had intellectual, adult attention and books and excellent health – but she was never assertive enough to be any good at making friends her own age. Friendships, if they came, were thrust upon her, not chosen. A brother or sister would have helped but Dad had a vasectomy after she was born – which was explained to her, with diagrams – so most of her hours outside school were spent alone or in the company of adults, usually clever ones with limited social skills. Hence, perhaps, her ready acceptance of tribal life at Summerglades.

She had never forgotten her bouts of sick terror when she went up to Oxford. Aggressively shy, she studied hard because anything else involved socializing. Weeks had passed before she realized nobody would notice in so big an organization if she had no friends, and nobody would care. And she lowered her guard, which was how Amber and Tris came to annex her.

It transpired that relations with her mother's family weren't entirely severed after all. Or possibly they merely slipped down below the level of male radar, to an occasional exchange of postcards or Christmas letters between mother and daughter. Laura was never introduced to her uncles or grandparents and, prompted by her father, tended to think of them, if she thought of them at all, as the Enemy. When her grandfather died, Mummy only broke the news after taking herself off to Itchen Abbas for the funeral. Laura and Dad surprised her at the kitchen table in her best dark suit and court shoes, with pink eyes, the order of service and her father's old watch. After that she took to slipping down to Hampshire for lunch roughly once a month, something Dad hated but was powerless to stop. Mummy at least respected the way things stood and didn't press very hard for Laura to join her. Laura was in her late teens, studying like fury for Oxbridge and reliably bolshie.

'She'd love to see you, you know,' was all Mummy said. 'Aren't you curious? She's your only surviving grandparent, after all.'

'She's never wanted to see me before,' was all Laura said. 'Why should I suddenly want to see her?' and the subject was closed.

She was thirty and living in Paris when Dad died, just months into a reluctant redundancy. Mummy was more or less retired by then, no longer supervising any PhD students, a resentful sort of consultant on a couple of research projects, nothing more. Within the year she had sold the house in Ripplevale Grove and moved to Winchester and this house, dumping or selling virtually every article of furniture in the old place and furnishing her new one with things inherited from the unmarried antique dealer brother, who had died. Any gaps were then filled with leavings of her mother's when her mother elected to sell the family house in Itchen Abbas and move to a tiny flat in a gracious sheltered housing development in Kingsworthy.

These pictures and furniture, elegant, discreet, what Mummy bluntly called *good*, were all Laura would ever know of the family she had refused to meet. It was all beautiful in its very English way, but when Mummy died, Laura decided, she would probably keep the book garages but sell every stick of the rest.

She started awake, glanced at her clock and saw she had barely nodded off but she forced herself upright just the same. It was a condition of living with her mother that she was tired all the time, forever nodding off in armchairs or at her desk, as though the sleepiness of old age were contagious. There were thirty-five years between them – compared to Mummy she should be an amazon – and yet it was Mummy, increasingly, who seemed the livelier one, the one keenest to be up and doing. 'Perhaps I'm sickening,' she thought. 'Perhaps I'm clinically depressed?'

As if affirming the point, came the clunk of her mother flopping down on the stair-lift seat followed by the descending buzz of its motor.

Laura crossed to the bathroom and gave her teeth a quick brush to rid her mouth of staleness. Her mother was without vanity so the bathroom mirror was pleasantly small, soap-splashed and badly lit. It was easy to avoid meeting one's eye as one brushed, rinsed and spat.

GLASS OF WATER

Something in his drug-company sandwich had brought on a thirst. Ben downed a glass of water at his sink then filled it and carried it back to his desk and drank the rest of it there. Like the other rooms where he worked, this one was bald of personal touches – no photographs, no possessions, nothing he couldn't carry out again in his bag or pockets – he had taken such a tumble in status in order to work here that he simply worked wherever the nurses put him.

Whichever half of the day wasn't devoted to the GUM clinic was given over to the separate HIV one. Fifteen years ago the two would have shared premises and appointment hours but this had never really been appropriate. Of course, new patients were often identified as a result of an HIV test conducted as part of a standard STD screening or treatment but HIV positive patients, whether they were still asymptomatic or had become ill were, thank God, usually long-term ones these days, requiring at least regular blood tests and check-ups to monitor their T cell levels and whatever drugs cocktail they were on, whereas a patient with syphilis might come to the GUM clinic just once in a lifetime.

Most of the HIV patients were sufficiently relaxed not to use pseudonyms. They were being seen regularly and doctors and staff in the department had won their confidence, but there were always exceptions: the man terrified he would lose his life insurance if word somehow got out, the woman Ben had seen only that afternoon, who he suspected was still keeping her HIV status from her husband and children.

So it was no surprise to glance down to his next appointment and find a Mrs Jones listed. Usually the patient's notes were enough to jog his memory or at least give him enough information not to cause offence through ignorance. But this Mrs Jones had no notes, only a pristine folder, on which a paperclipped slip declared her a *new pt*, with a blank sheet of A4 inside it. Ben finished his water then buzzed the nurses' station.

'Hi, Sherry. Mrs Jones who's due in next. Is she a transfer?'

'Hang on, Ben.' Sherry could be heard conferring with a colleague. 'Yup,' she said. 'No notes. She's a fresh referral, just moved to the area.'

'Ah. Okay.'

He stepped outside and walked along the short corridor to the waiting area. This doubled as the reception area for the adjacent HIV ward so was always fairly busy with visitors calling in or waiting to take discharged patients home. He dodged a toddler who was stomping in pursuit of a jingling rubber ball and scanned the faces. 'Mrs Jones?'

It was her. Of course it was. She stood, suppressing a smile and shook his offered hand.

How could he ever have thought she was funny-looking? With her honey-brown limbs and long neck she was lovely to him now, and the shy way she ducked her head slightly as she met his eye so that her hair shaded her face made him want to kiss her on the spot. 'This way, please,' he told her and led the way around the corner and along the corridor back to his room. He never spoke to patients until they were safely inside, to protect their confidentiality, but this was impossible with her. He had to say something. Words were bubbling up and he struggled to make them appropriate as colleagues and nurses were everywhere.

'We've no notes for you yet,' he stammered.

'No,' she said, her voice similarly wavery. 'I've moved here unexpectedly. From Paris.'

'Paris? That explains it. In here please.'

He had barely closed the door than she was kissing him. By some delicious miracle the door had a lock.

'I'm sorry,' she murmured, coming up for air. 'So sorry.'

'No,' he said. 'It's me. It's all me. Such a coward. I'm. Oh. I'm …' And they had to kiss more. It was intolerable not to.

135

'How long have we …?' she began

'Fifteen minutes,' he said. 'Absolute max. We really shouldn't.'

But with a couple of quick, efficient gestures she had undone her dress and stepped out of it. She had on dark green French lingerie he remembered from an earlier date. It was impossibly predictable and corny of him but he found it deeply exciting. 'Oh Christ,' he said. 'Hang on,' he said and dropped the blinds. They were high up but window cleaners had a way of appearing unannounced.

She was clambering onto the examination couch. Her bare feet squeaked on its vinyl upholstery.

'This is so bad,' he whispered.

'I know.' She smiled and put up a hand to stop him undoing his tie. 'No,' she muttered. 'No time. Keep everything on.'

It was all over in five minutes or less. She was on fire and he barely had to touch her. A cleaner had unknowingly released the brake on the couch wheels and their rocking moved it some distance. As he tidied himself up she slipped back into her dress and shoes and sat demurely in the chair she'd have taken as a patient, and repaired her hair with a comb. He sat before her and took one of her hands between his and kissed its fingertips.

'Oh God,' he said.

'I know,' she said.

'Paris, eh?'

'Yup.'

'You'd better ...'

'Go. Yes. I know.'

'But can I see you?'

'Yes. Oh yes. Don't be silly. No more nonsense.'

'No. I'll ... We'll ...'

She reclaimed her hand, briefly cupped his jaw in it and stood. 'Of course we will. Everything.'

'Everything's going to be fine, isn't it?'

'Yes.'

She kissed his brow then let herself out. He twisted the blind control and the sunlight fell back in harsh bands. Then he refilled his water glass and drained it. Before he washed his hands in lurid pink Hibiscrub, he raised his fingers to his mouth and nose and breathed and, hot water steaming the mirror before him, let out a kind of sob then cleared his throat and pretended to cough.

TEA

'You slept too,' her mother said.

'I didn't mean to.'

Mummy reached up and gently patted the back of Laura's head. 'Hair standing up a bit,' she said.

These moments of solicitude or tenderness between them were becoming more common but were still so unusual, so out of character, that Laura did not know how to deal with them. 'Shall we have tea in the garden?' she said. 'I bought a lemon drizzle cake at the WI.'

'Oh good.'

Having never seen the point of sweets or baking, having raised little Laura on a scrupulously healthy and frugal diet, Mummy had developed a childishly sweet tooth in her old age. Laura had to buy her several chocolate bars in the weekly shop which Mummy evidently ate in secret, as they were never shared. Occasionally Laura would find squares lost down the sides of chairs or backs of pillows and, if unobserved, would eat them swiftly and without compunction. She suspected she was putting on weight.

Mummy had already laboriously set tea things on a tray. Laura put the kettle on to boil then hurried out ahead of her to bank up her wooden garden seat with the pile of cushions stacked by the door for just this purpose.

'I was looking for something in my tights drawer when I found a box of stuff. Junk really. Photographs and so on. It's by the breadbin. Keep what you want and we can chuck the rest.' As was her wont, Mummy carried on talking as she walked slowly into the garden and out of range. 'And talking of chucking, we should clear half the things out of that drawer. I'm never going to wear tights again, just hideous knee-highs, so one might as well ...' She said something about making tree ties then her words became indistinct.

'Can't hear you,' Laura said, too quietly to be heard herself, and she lifted the lid of the box – an old Terry's *1767* one – and began to pick through the contents. There were holiday photographs that had all been left out of the albums for some reason. Laura with her father, smiling, bearded and now crazily young-looking, in front of Christchurch Priory, and with her mother at Wimborne Minster. Laura's parents photographed lopsidedly by Laura, beaming on either side of a seaside donkey in a straw hat. Laura on her own, aged about six, in a Ladybird jersey and trousers with little elasticated straps under the feet, looking tense and isolated in an expanse of anonymous grass. Then there were several buttons and toggles to longlost garments and a conference badge announcing Professor Harriet Jellicoe. There was a picture of her and Dad looking glum beside the Arsénal canal and several holiday postcards from illegible friends, inexplicably retained.

As the kettle whistled, she tossed the lot in the rubbish bin and made their tea and set slices of cake on plates. Then she retrieved the box from among the kitchen scraps to take out the small photographs of her father looking young and of her smaller self, of solemn Lara, which she tucked into her pocket before carrying the tray out to the garden.

The sun had been shining all day so their little oasis was rich with the scents of sunbaked lavender and sweet pea. Bees were becoming noisily drunk in two great potted stands of candidum lilies in pots that framed the sitting area. Mummy was ever more reliant on pot gardening to create her effects since it involved less stooping and merely required Laura to move the pots about. A rotating quartet of pots in the same place had already seen dwarf daffodils and anemone blanda give way to delft blue hyacinths and green and white parrot tulips. Autumn would bring acidanthera and nerines, whose strong shade of pink always gave concern. Winter ushered in a quieter, longer display from winter pansies and a variegated ivy or two.

Mummy sat in dappled shade with her mottled, still skinny legs on what had been a gardener's kneeler but now served as a footstool. With her pretty frock and hair recently brushed and sitting in a kind of bower, she might have been an advertisement for a retirement bond or geriatric emergency support. *Mrs Lewis can rest assured. Can you?* Only she was Professor Jellicoe and was reading a gruesomely illustrated book called *Plagues of Venus* she was reviewing for the *TLS*, which made the image a little less cosy.

Laura poured their tea and passed cake, which Mummy ate at once, shedding yellow crumbs across her open book.

'Did you find the box?'

'Rubbish mainly.'

'Thought so.'

Laura handed her the photograph of herself on the expanse of grass. 'Where was this?'

Mummy stared at it. 'God knows,' she said. 'Could have been anywhere. If you find the album with you at that age you could probably match the clothes and work it out that way.' She looked at the picture again. 'You were such a *serious* little girl.'

'I had pretty serious parents.'

Mummy handed the picture back without comment, brushed the crumbs off her book and continued to read. 'Is there any more cake?' she asked.

'Of course,' Laura said and fetched it. She knew it was irritating asking questions of someone trying to read but she didn't care. She had fetched the cake, she had earned the right. 'Did you regret it, ever: your relationship with Dad?'

Mummy carried on reading as she answered, an old trick, like broaching tricky subjects when driving. 'Of course not. He saved me. My father was of that generation that would only give up a daughter to another man, whatever they thought of him, not to a career.' She laid the book on her lap thoughtfully. 'I feel guilty sometimes, of course. Your father would have been happier with a more womanly woman.'

'No!'

'He wanted far more children. Maybe to make up for his lack of family. For all his disapproving talk about patriarchy, deep down he'd have liked a tribe but I wasn't one of nature's mothers. Not really.' She caught Laura with her cool, patrician gaze. 'Was I?'

'I had no points of comparison,' Laura said and looked away to watch a thrush that was hunting through a flowerbed. It pounced on a snail and threw it hard against the wall.

'Do you want to go to Evensong later? I mean, would you mind?' Mummy asked.

'Not at all. I'll drive us down at five.'

'You've got hardly any work done today. I'm sorry. Tomorrow can be more peaceful.'

'That's all right. No. It was simply that I was lying on my bed just now looking at the furniture and I realized that, apart from the book garages, which were always yours in any case, you didn't keep anything from Ripplevale Grove.'

'All that awful pine!'

'But you lived with it for decades.'

'I had to. We were poor and it was cheap. After a while I stopped seeing it. But after he died, and I was retired, I started seeing it again and without him it wasn't very bearable. Or London. Lara, it was only tables and chairs.'

'Laura.'

'Laura. I think of him often. Every day. Don't you?'

'Probably.'

'What's happened to that nice man who came by? The one like the sexy BBC man with the gap in his teeth. I liked him.'

'So did I. Oh. You know. It's complicated when you're grown up. More tea?'

Mummy shook her head, glanced at her father's watch and returned to the plagues of Venus.

So. Ben had at last been mentioned, made a topic of conversation. Laura continued to think of him as she set their tea things back on the tray, carried them back to the house, put away the cake and loaded the dishwasher. Her thoughts began to overwhelm her.

She hurried up to her room, closed the door, kicked off her shoes and lay on her bed, just for a moment. She rolled onto her front, pressing her fists into her groin. She felt his weight above her, his voice at her ear and cried out into the depths of her pillow.

LOVE LETTER

Darling. You always said – you probably don't remem-
ber – we should never call each other that because it's
what people call lovers they no longer love. So I'm sorry
but I like it. I like its sturdy Saxon feel. Would deorling
be less offensive? (Don't be impressed – just looked that
up on the net.)

Your wonderful little visit to find me at work, totally
unlooked for, unhoped for, unearned, has sent my mood
rocketing and sod work, blow patients, I want to share
it with you. You know I'm hopeless on the phone and not
much better at explaining myself face to face. There are
already several versions of this torn up in the office bin
and still I'm stumbling.

We couldn't talk when you visited but perhaps that
was a good thing if it stopped me blurting things that
should be said with care. But now that I've had a while
to think everything seems so clear, so simple suddenly,

as if you'd blown the clouds away and all the shades of grey were gone.

I love you and I want to be with you always, whatever it takes and whatever compromises or sacrifices that involves me in and mess that means wading through.

Bobby will cope. He'll adjust and cope, of course he will. It's taken this time of worry and not talking to make me see I had my priorities in a twist and I've been crazily overprotective of him. Change is a part of living and he has to get used to it if he's to have independence.

But all of this assumes agreement on your part. Typical male bloody arrogance, I can hear you say. My behaviour has offered you an insult that would perfectly entitle you to tell me to bog off. Oh but I hope you won't. Can you ever forgive me? Can we somehow not forget but draw a line, at least, and start again? Christ, I hope so.

I probably won't post this, my deorling. I think I'm too shy. Either that or I'm just rehearsing on paper, building up my courage for the things I need to tell you. I love you and all will be well. All my love. Absolutely all of it. Bx

EVENSONG

It was a perfect evening, a sky of intense blue, swifts swooping down across the Close's lawns after flies, a handful of the local youth, blasted by cider and sun, flopped across one another beneath the lime trees.

Laura parked in a disabled space by the long run of flying buttresses along the great nave's southern flank. She could hear the choir rehearsing in a nearby chamber as she unfolded her mother's walker and rolled it up to the passenger door.

Scorning as ever to go into the cathedral with the tourists and face embarrassment at the begging boxes – which, in any case, represented a big detour if one was aiming for the quire – Mummy struck out for the passage called the Slype where a sort of service entrance was tucked away from public view. She had once stood behind one of the canons as he let them both in there and had memorized the code for the lock, OISJBN850H, as a mnemonic.

'Once I was 16. Joy! But now am 85. Oh Hell!' she told herself as she punched letters and digits into a little pad. And in they went, through the south transept, past the angels kneeling around the Wilberforce tomb and up the steps to the quire by the quickest route. There was a wheelchair lift but Mummy disliked that as it was on the far side of the building, and preferred to tug herself up the stairs by the handrail while Laura walked close beside her just in case, carrying the walker.

They were greeted by a sideswoman as though they were regulars, which perhaps they had become by now, and found themselves seats, thrones effectively, in the choir stalls. Laura still found it hard to believe that such splendid, ancient seats, just feet from choir and clergy and each a museum piece, were available to the public. She looked around her defensively, prepared as ever for some verger or official to move them on.

Religion had played no part, good or bad, in her life until now. She was raised in carefully scientific godlessness and sent to schools where RE was judiciously ecumenical and thus deeply confusing and dull. Apart from the most obvious, primary school bits like Adam and Eve, Jonah and the Whale or David and Goliath, she was quite unfamiliar with the Bible, especially with its New Testament, her school in Camden having been eager not to offend its Jewish constituency. So she had always felt disadvantaged visiting art galleries and churches on holiday because so much of the painting and sculpture was a literature she could barely read.

Slipping into Evensong, like good quality chocolate biscuits and George II side tables, was one of the luxurious tastes Mummy had acquired in widowhood. She claimed she had simply been exploring the cathedral one afternoon during her first year in the city when the service was announced. She was making her way to one of the exits along with the other flustered godless when the choir began singing an introit. The beauty of the music forced her to take a seat to listen, if only from a distance. She had come back several afternoons after that, always sitting well outside the quire so she could enjoy the music and words but not feel implicated in the act of worship.

'But then I thought, *This is silly. Who am I so scared of? I don't care what people think; my faith or lack of it is entirely my affair.*'

So she took to sitting in the quire with everyone else and soon discovered one didn't have to sit in the boring modern chairs towards the altar but could sit in the stalls, on tough tapestry cushions, above exquisite misericords, and while away the service's drier intervals admiring the carvings on every side – oak huntsmen, animals, leaves and fruit. She remained in her seat for the prayers, but then, looking around, she saw that kneeling was beyond many of the older worshippers and beneath the dignity of many of the younger ones. She stood for the creed, however, with everyone else.

When Laura first attended with her she was astounded at this. 'But it's mumbo-jumbo!'

'Yes.'

'But you know all the words!'

'Of course. I was a nicely-brought-up girl. I attended confirmation classes at St Swithun's for a year when I was twelve and was confirmed at thirteen, by the Bishop of Winchester in this very cathedral.'

'But you don't believe it now?'

'I'm not sure I believed it then. I was just being obedient. You got confirmed in the same spirit that you got married, in the fond hope that something solid would follow on the heels of faith. And since I don't believe, I don't see the harm in saying the words. They're nice words. Certainty is so reassuring. And it seems courteous, somehow, like joining in a native custom. If we were in a Hindu temple or among Zoroastrians, I expect I'd try to fall in with whatever they were doing in the same way. To be polite. The music and the building are so beautiful it seems a cheap enough offering in return.'

Laura did her best to remain her father's daughter. She looked pointedly about her or even read inappropriate parts of the prayer book or cathedral pamphlets during the prayers and remained staunchly seated when all around her stood and faced east for the creed. But it was hard. She didn't like people staring, didn't like to draw attention to herself. And, for all his brave words about bigotry and patriarchy and opiate of the masses, her father never faced the enemy on home ground. So she compromised and took to standing and facing east like everyone else, but kept her silence and resisted the cowardly urge to move her lips and did not rise to Mummy's mischievous offer to teach her the words.

'I could teach you the Catechism too. I tested myself when I couldn't sleep the other night and found I can still remember it all.'

Creed aside, it was a wonderfully undemanding ritual, almost a concert. The music varied hugely, from sparse polyphonic or even plainchant settings used on nights when only men's voices were available through lush Victorian settings and turn of the century tearjerkers to challenging contemporary ones. There was no tedious sermon, no tub-thumping hymn. After several exposures, Laura found she was enjoying the psalms, with their frequent bouts of despair or indignation, and the unexpected charms of the readings. Much of it meant nothing to her but she still found she could appreciate it, much as she had appreciated displays in the Institut du Monde Arabe without understanding a word of Arabic script.

At that time of year she enjoyed looking up from her magnificent seat to explore the farther reaches of vaulting and tracery with her eyes. In the winter months there was a different pleasure to be had from the vast darkness of the church around them and the sense of the quire as a pool of light in a forest of nocturnal stone.

The words, especially those of the nunc dimittis and the repeated references to night and stillness – *the busy world is hushed, the fever of life is over* – the inevitable identification of the end of the day with the end of life, tended to bring on a curious fit of nostalgia or species of homesickness, a dwelling on chances past and friends lost, that could make her tearful if she didn't guard against it.

Tonight, inspired by her thoughts of his rejected furniture and the box of old photographs she had so casually discarded, she found herself thinking about her father and when she had last seen him alive. She touched a hand to her shirt pocket and was reassured to feel his picture in there.

He had marked the early weeks of his 'voluntary' redundancy by catching the Eurostar to visit her in Paris. It was a tremendous bother at the time, as she was involved in a messy love affair with a divorced client who was trying to get serious just when she was preparing to ditch him. Her apartment was tiny – not suited to guests who needed a bedroom of their own. She slept on the sofa so that Dad could have her room, and gave up three days to show him the city which, astonishingly, he had never visited.

She had never spent so long with him without her mother, and the things about him and her parents' relationship the visit threatened to reveal made her nervous and tetchy. There was a limit to how much sightseeing she could make him do and at regular intervals they had to sit on park benches or at café tables and he would talk. More disturbingly he would ask direct questions, like how was she, no but really, in herself. And did she have someone special at the moment. And then there would be heavy sighs, which she knew were partly his way of showing he knew she was holding back the truth from him but also her cue to ask him things in turn. It was a cue she harshly overlooked to talk brightly about what they would do next.

Looking back she wondered if he had already known he was ill, if he had been settling emotional accounts. The classic behaviour for a living husband in such a position would surely have been to wring some kind of assurance from her that she would look after her widowed mother. Instead he seemed to be implying that he had learnt things, sad lessons, he wished he had known at her age. But she spent the visit parrying and deflecting his conversational advances and masking herself emotionally.

It had been very odd. When there were three of them as a family, her instinct, her role almost, had always been to take his part. *Poor Dad. Overlooked. Undervalued.* But without her mother there as a mock adversary, so much brighter than either of them, so much more assured, the polarity shifted and she found herself reacting as though he were a sort of predator on her feelings.

And then he dropped dead on an Underground escalator, only weeks after his visit.

Of course, what he had been trying to say, she suspected now, was, *Are you lonely? I don't want you to be lonely because I still am and it's a terrible thing.*

Her automatic view of her childhood, her account for others at dinner tables, was that she had been the inter-loper, the infant gooseberry, in a great, unmarried love story. It was a story she still told herself because it was a comfort and required nothing of her: that he had come from the wrong side of the tracks and saved a brilliant woman from a stultifying future. From things she let slip, it was a story her mother told herself too. But the truth was possibly sadder: that he had indeed offered an escape route but that, once escaped into their unconventional ménage, she left him behind. It was never pretended he was her intellectual equal. He never rose above the level of lecturer, and that at a lowly polytechnic. He was never invited to conferences, never asked to contribute articles to *New Society* or *Tribune*.

For her mother, research was all. Her obsession with proving or disproving the existence of prions, for instance; teaching was something she always regarded as a necessary evil, secondary to the formation and super-vision of a team of research students. Whereas he loved his students, clearly, and relished his role as a sensible, avuncular mentor in their messy, risky lives. For him they were, undoubtedly, the extra children he couldn't have – a demanding, exasperating, extended family – and being eased out of their midst by his employers must have been shattering to him, a huge bereavement.

And now her mother had all but erased him from the picture. He lived on in bits of Laura, of course, in the photograph albums and, oddly, in the one thing he had given Mummy beside an escape route: the freedom she felt in shedding her clothes.

The anthem that evening was a chunk of the Brahms *German Requiem*, rendered into clumsily Teutonic English: *How Lovely Are Thy Dwellings Fair*. Laura was just thinking how pootling the accompaniment sounded reduced to an organ from the full, rich orchestration when there was a loud sniff from Mummy followed by a frantic scrabbling in pockets. She was doing her best not to cry. Another, fruitier sniff followed.

Laura had a clean handkerchief on her and passed her that. Mummy took it. Her face was hidden by the outcrop of carved oak between them but she patted Laura's thigh in thanks.

Once they were all standing to let the choir and clergy process out and then variously kneeling or slumping or bowing heads for whatever improvised prayer people felt obliged to offer up by way of a private closing paragraph, she seemed herself again.

They shook the hands of a smiley canon, were greeted, without handshakes, by the Dean and once again Laura held the walker while Mummy made heavy use of the long, time-smoothed handrail.

'I'm fine,' she said in response to Laura's tentative enquiries once they were back out in the Slype. 'Bloody

Brahms, that's all. Pavlov's dog. I need a drink. Did you manage to buy another bag of those nice cheese straws at the WI?'

LOVING MEMORY

Blissed out, tie tugged loose and jacket over one shoulder because of the heat, Ben strolled down the Romsey Road and cut left to walk home under the trees across the top of Oram's Arbour. When not framing letters to Laura he had spent the afternoon having repeatedly to remind himself not to smile or laugh inappropriately as patients confided their stories or presented their symptoms. Finally he could see the way forward and the sense of freedom after days mired in guilt and uncertainty was as intoxicating as the June air.

A gang of children was playing a haphazard game of rounders on the grass, assisted by a demented, spring-heeled terrier which ran, barking, wherever the ball was pitched or struck, and attracting impotent glares and a few comments from commuters obliged to follow the path through the game's middle on their way to the station. The grass had been cut that afternoon and the Arbour was still full of its scent and the children's running feet and calves were spattered with it. Ben watched for a minute or two, enchanted, but soon moved on because children made him think about Chloë and he didn't want thoughts of her impinging on his happily irresponsible mood.

Bobby was waiting for him, smartly dressed, hands all but on hips in agitation.

'Come on,' he said. 'It starts in half an hour.'

'What does?'

'Shirley's thing. You'd forgotten.'

'Yes. Sorry. Damn.'

'Where are you going?'

'I've got to shower. I'm filthy from work.'

'No time!'

'Got to. Have a drink. I'll be ready in five minutes.'

He raced to the bathroom, cursing his midsummer languor on the way home. He had forgotten entirely, even though people from work would be going and had probably said things to remind him if only he had been paying attention.

Bobby knew Shirley because she'd been the volunteer teacher who finally dragged him through his English and Maths GCSEs in his early twenties. She was one of Winchester's very few HIV patients to die in recent memory, discounting those who died in accidents or of other illnesses. Most responded well to antiretroviral therapy. Even patients only brought onto the drugs in the late stages of full-blown AIDS tended to display a dramatically quick improvement in immunity. Most treated at an earlier stage soon had HIV viral loads that were undetectable and CD4 counts that were little below normal. Shirley might have done better had she been diagnosed earlier but she was an old school radical and when her husband died from AIDS, well before the antiretrovirals were available, she had flatly refused an HIV test out of a kind of solidarity. And she had continued to do so, insisting she was fine and that she preferred to assume she was HIV positive than to risk being told she wasn't and so feel excluded from her husband's fate. Finally diagnosed with AIDS when what she had taken for seasonal flu turned into a nasty bout of pneumonia, she then proved to be one of the extremely rare cases to respond poorly to antiretrovirals. They tried her with a different *drug cocktail*, as she gleefully put it, but her T cell count continued to sink. Then she had succumbed to cerebral lymphoma and died in just three weeks.

In the early days of HIV it was a given that the staff on AIDS wards had to unlearn some of their training in professional detachment. They saw the same patients in extremis off and on over such a long period it was impossible not to become at least a little involved emotionally and the patients and their loved ones came to expect it. There was far less professional trauma now than when the wards seemed to offer nothing but death or death postponed, so Shirley's death had rattled everyone.

'Okay,' Ben called down, dashing from bathroom to bedroom in his towel. 'Nearly there!'

He grabbed smartish weekend clothes. Shirley was wildly informal and would have found nothing wrong in his attending a memorial service in open-necked shirt and a linen jacket instead of stifling in his work suit as Bobby would surely do. He stamped into shoes, snatched up his car keys and bounded down the narrow stairs. 'Ready! Bobby?' There was no sign of him. 'Bob?' he called back up the stairs to Bobby's room then saw him coming in from the street. 'Where'd you get to?'

'Nowhere,' Bobby said but he was smiling wickedly.

'What have you been doing?'

'Nothing!' Bobby grinned even more. He had never been able to keep secrets because of his tendency to smile when under tension.

'Okay. Come on or we'll really be late.'

The car had been driven so rarely lately its windows were streaked with dust and debris from the trees. Ben had forgotten to fill the windscreen wash bottle so using the wipers only made their view more smeary. He drove as fast as he dared, peering between the patches of murk while Bobby sang to himself.

St Cross was a village, or former village, on the other side of Winchester and the city centre had a one-way system that would have taken far too long to navigate at that time of day, so Ben drove them onto the Romsey Road then headed right to the edge of the hospital campus before driving left down St James Lane and onto a series of well heeled residential streets that led out to the south. Which meant they had to turn right outside Professor Jellicoe's house.

Cars were coming uphill so they were obliged to wait a moment or two.

'I've got to know the people that live in there,' Ben ventured.

'In there?' Bobby said, looking across at the wall and gate. 'I've always liked the look of that place. Really private. What's it like inside?'

'Lovely. The old lady's a naturist.'

'Oh. What's that?'

'She likes leaving all her clothes off. That's why she lives there.'

'That's so cool. Is she your friend?'

'Er. No. I know her daughter, Laura.'

'Oh. You can turn now, Ben.'

'Oh yeah. So I can.'

Parking in St Cross was usually a challenge but so many people were expected that permission had been given for cars to park in a nearby field. A couple of jolly women in bright pink were stationed on the turning down to the church with signs saying *Shirley's Send-Off This Way!!* They waved Ben through a gate in the fence.

It was a handsome old church, much of it Norman, and from some angles looked almost like the cathedral in miniature. It formed the centrepiece of St Cross Hospital, the almshouse foundation immortalized by Trollope, open to widowers and bachelors of the diocese. The ringing of bells, the old gateways and quadrangles, cloistered walk and sunny terraces and general air of rosebushed ease put Ben in mind of an Oxford college and touched his good mood with sweet regret. He resolved to bring Laura on a walk down there, perhaps across the water meadows to a nearby pub, next time they were both free.

People were still arriving so they weren't quite the last. Ben saw several men in pink or lilac shirts and had yet to spot a woman in funereal colours.

'Is there a theme going on with the clothes?' he asked.

'Shirley liked pink.'

'Shirley was blind.'

'She liked the way it sounded.'

Bobby, he noticed now, had changed since that morning into a shell-pink shirt and a dove-grey silk tie with pink spots. 'You might have warned me,' he said.

'No point. You've got nothing pink to wear. I looked.'

It was a large church and two thirds full. They were handed service sheets and took seats towards the back. Ben saw three of the nurses from the ward there, all in pink tops, and one of the doctors, who he was relieved to see was looking flushed in sober work clothes. He knew no one else. Bobby, however, seemed to know lots of people and was much waved at. While he left the pew to hug someone, Ben focussed on the service sheet.

There was a photograph on the front of Shirley on the day of her wedding to the bisexual geography teacher from whom she had contracted HIV. Her guide dog stood between them, his harness handle decorated with flowers. The husband had been among the unlucky ones, like Laura's Tris, who sickened and died in the early Eighties. By the time Ben first became aware of Shirley she was very much the merry widow, as galvanized into AIDS activism by bereavement as she had once been goaded by blindness into campaigning on behalf of people with disabilities.

Ben glanced at the hymns to reassure himself he knew them then looked around him. Never having been to Lourdes or Knock, he had never seen so many wheelchairs in one church. Or walking sticks. Or guide dogs. Perhaps as a tribute to Shirley, those with guide dogs had been encouraged to sit on either side of the central aisle so their dogs, all of them impeccably behaved and sitting upright beside their owner's chairs, formed a kind of guard of honour for the priest as she walked to the front to welcome everyone and announce the first hymn.

Bobby stopped socializing and dodged back to his seat as the organ struck up with *All Things Bright and Beautiful*.

'How do you know all these people?' Ben asked him.

'I dunno,' Bobby said. 'I live here, don't I?' And he started to sing, vigorously, slightly out of key and not letting his difficulty in keeping up with the words on the page get in the way of a good tune. After *Lord God made them all* he gave up on Mrs Alexander, gave up trying to sing words he couldn't remember and merely sang *La La La* to the verses and rejoined the text for each chorus, which caused several of their neighbours to turn round and smile.

Ben was happy to see he was no longer suffering from his little problem. Knowing Bobby, he would not have trusted the insecticide to work on a single application and would have been reapplying at restless intervals throughout the day and was probably feeling a little scorched down below.

The priest entered her pulpit during the last verse and, once there was silence, invited them all to sit. 'Don't worry,' she went on. 'I know how fond Shirley was of a good party so this won't take long.' There was a flurry of laughter. 'Our friend, Shirley Burgess,' she went on, 'was an extraordinary woman. Confined to a wheelchair until her late teens, totally blind all her life, she changed more lives and made more friendships in a year than most of us could hope to do in a lifetime. Yes, she suffered when she was losing Paul and yes, she suffered towards the end of her long battle with the effect of the HIV virus but if I had to choose one word to typify Shirley it would be *Undefeated*. It will come as no surprise to anyone who knew her that she left nothing unplanned for her memorial service and certainly wasn't going to trust a mere priest to organize it. That hymn we just sang, and every word you hear until I get my way and say some prayers at the very end, was chosen by her as her loving message to all of you. None of you was at her funeral because she insisted that be a completely private affair and because, as she kept repeating to any of us in earshot, "The death bit is completely unimportant."'

The priest sat down and the lower lectern was approached by an extremely old blind man Ben didn't know but often saw being led down the high street by his dog. Dog at his side now, he fumbled noisily to ascertain where the microphone was, raised a laugh by saying, 'Sorry, Shirley,' then produced a sheet of Braille. 'The first reading is from the words of Henry Scott Holland,' he said, 'who was a canon of St Paul's Cathedral and died in 1918.' He then turned his head from side to side in that way the sightless do when gathering in an audience. 'Death is nothing at all,' he began. 'I have only slipped into the next room. I am I and you are you. Whatever we were to each other, that we are still.'

Ben listened just long enough to recognize the passage as one their mother had chosen for her own funeral. He glanced at Bobby but he was simply listening, the way he tended to, with his head a little on one side. (Mum always worried this meant that he might be deaf, although his hearing was only slightly below average.) The choice of reading had surprised Ben because it was so forthright in its avowal of an afterlife and he never thought their mother had believed in such things. But death weakened many resolves and perhaps she simply wanted to, or died hoping.

A local handbell group performed next. In the echoing acoustic, their ringing seemed merely loud and blurred at first but then Ben realized he was hearing a sort of introduction. The melody, when it emerged, was *Climb Ev'ry Mountain*, which raised many knowing smiles and tumultuous applause at its end. There was another hymn, *Lord of the Dance*, whose words had always made Ben cringe. Bobby laughed out loud at the verse that rhymed *whipped* and *stripped*. Then a Scotswoman in a wheelchair declaimed Mary Frye's *Do Not Stand at my Grave and Weep*, which drew murmurs of appreciation. And then, to Ben's surprise, Bobby stood, walked solemnly to the lectern and began to speak, his voice a little shaky with nerves at first.

'Shirley taught me,' he told them all. 'She got me through my GCSEs in Maths and English. Finally! So I could get a job selling coffees and papers instead of just washing up and putting out rubbish bags. Being taught English by someone who does all her reading with her fingers was very ...' He broke off, searching for a word. 'Was very humbling. I think Shirley wanted me to read this poem because I had to write an essay on it and I really, really hated writing essays.'

There was kind laughter, which he joined in, and a few people, who presumably knew they were brothers, glanced round at Ben. Bobby reached into his jacket pocket and produced a piece of paper which he unfolded. '*First Sight*,' he announced, 'by Philip Larkin.' He took an audible breath in and out and in again then started. 'Lambs that learn to walk in snow …'

He still didn't find reading easy or pleasurable and, as always, he had to follow the words with a pointing finger so as not to lose his place, which made for an unintended caesura between lines as his finger travelled from the end of one to the start of the next. So *Meet a vast unwelcome, know Nothing but a sunless glare* came out with a new sense as *Meet a vast unwelcome "No!" Nothing but a …* He had clearly been rigorously coached, by Shirley presumably, with a tapping of her thickly ringed hand on a tabletop, in the idea of metre – *AS they WAIT beSIDE the EWE* – which rather overwhelmed Larkin's understated evocation of wonder, and Bobby's recitation nearly broke down altogether, faced with the challenge of *immeasurable*. But it was astonishing and Ben wished their mother could have lived to see it.

Shirley, wise old bird, had known exactly the effect her combination of reader and poem would have and Bobby walked back up the aisle, still seraphic in his thirties, beaming with proud relief, to antiphonal nose-blows. The organ was playing for the last hymn, accompanied now by the handbells to make a big finish and, standing with the rest, Ben stepped outside the row to let Bobby back in and was greeted with a bear hug and a wave of his brother's woody-sweet cologne.

The hymn was *Be Thou My Vision* and, while Bobby la la'd gutsily at his side, Ben found himself thinking not just of their mother but of Laura and Chloë and the mess he had made, and was about to make, of both their lives and of all the time he had so foolishly wasted, time for the building of memories and the getting and raising of children, and of all the good that might yet be wrested from the wreckage. He found himself completely unmanned and had to fumble for a handkerchief and sit down long before the last of the bells had jangled.

DRINKS

The weather had changed in their hour in the cathedral. Clouds had rolled in and the air, so honeyed earlier, had become prickly and oppressive. There was a rumble of thunder as Mummy was shuffling to the car. She had taken to buying *going-out shoes* a size too big for her as they were easier to get on and off, and they clacked on the tarmac as she progressed. 'Storm coming,' she said with approval. She liked storms; the more crackly and electrical the better.

Laura had been terrified of lightning as a child and no amount of placid statistics from Dad or explanation from Mummy of the positive and negative charges on either side of a thundercloud helped. In vain they tried to make a storm fun by encouraging her to work out how far away the storm centre was based on thunder travelling at twelve miles a minute and lightning at one hundred and eighty-six thousand a second. Their well meaning efforts were undercut by their chuckles – they both loved storms and, Laura now suspected, were turned on by them like teenagers in a horror film – and by the simple fact that her fear lay beyond the reach of reason, like fear of flying. It was no use being told how unlikely it was to be struck down by a bolt from the blue. She was scared of the suddenness of lighting, its lack of rhythmic predictability and its silence. She had long ago learnt to hide her terror but she had never lost it.

A bossy girlfriend whisked her off to a great house party in the Cevennes once. Laura was the only un-attached female, the only unattached male was too young for her, too gay and sullenly in love with someone's husband, and there was a storm, quite the most violent summer storm she had ever shuddered through. She was no dog lover, had never overcome her disappoint-ment that there were even more dogs in Paris than in London. And the hosts had a Great Dane, an imperi-ous, black-splodged bitch called Célimène that wore a collar from Hermès and showed no interest in Laura until the storm began. Then, while everyone else whooped and shrieked and went swimming in the rain, Célimène sought her out, sensing a fellow sufferer. Laura had never seen an animal so afraid. The great beast lost all haughtiness as it cowered against her knees under the kitchen table, teeth chattering, tail beneath its legs. And in her self-conscious attempts to comfort it, Laura felt herself the mistress of her own fear by comparison.

As they drove back around the Close, out under its arched gate and back up St Swithun's Street, the skies grew darker and darker and the thunder and lightning became more frequent and closer together. Mummy wound her window down and breathed like a wine taster. 'It always smells fantastic just before summer rain,' she said. 'Don't you find? Jasmine and compost heaps.'

The rain began to fall as they were driving into the garage and by the time she had unlocked the gate and they had made their stately progress through the garden, their dresses were wet through.

She set the kettle to boil for couscous then hurried upstairs to towel her hair and put on something dry. It came as no surprise to come down to find Mummy's clothes left in a damp heap at the foot of the stairs and to see her in the garden, pottering back and forth with a pair of secateurs and a ball of twine. She was tying back flowers the rain threatened to topple over and deadheading where necessary, but she was also delighting in the simple animal pleasure of feeling a summer downpour coursing over her skin.

Laura paused in mixing her mother's gin and tonic and pouring herself a glass of wine, to watch and marvel. She could not imagine reaching eighty, a whole thirty-five years hence, and facing the inevitable rebellion of her body, everything stretching and heading south and dewlaps and wattles and wrinkles and greyness, yet still taking pleasure in something so entirely commonplace

181

and physical. The old woman before her presented such a red-blooded contrast to all the walking-sticked worshippers in the cathedral earlier, seemingly united in a retreat from the body into things of the spirit.

There was no point taking her out a drink as the rain would dilute it in seconds, so Laura simply made sure there was a bath towel at the ready for her return indoors then set about making their supper. She tossed a handful of frozen peas into dry couscous then poured hot water and a little olive oil over them and shredded a mixture of dried apricot, pistachios, spring onion and mint while she waited for the couscous to rehydrate and the peas to thaw. Then she tossed a punnet of raspberries in vanilla sugar then slid a pair of lamb chops under the grill.

She was fond of food and eating but cooking bored her and years of living on a budget in a confined space had taught her to favour meals that were largely a matter of careful shopping and cunning assembly over menus that involved long oven hours and the production of lingering heat and smells.

While the chops began to sizzle, she turned on the radio in the hope of distraction from the storm. A Prom had started, which she normally enjoyed. But it was the broadcast of a new composition. She persevered for a minute or two but found it impossibly angular so she switched channels and made do with a soothingly impenetrable discussion on the relative psychological merits of a variety of spiritual disciplines.

A lightning flash lit the garden for a second and set the radio crackling and made her jump as though a gun had gone off. A great whump of thunder was followed by more lightning almost at once and all the power turned off and on again, which would mess up both their clock radios. She glanced anxiously through the open door. Mummy was looking more than ever like something from a radical *King Lear*, with leaves and petals sticking to her breasts and thighs and her hair flattened and darkened by the rain and a growing pile of clippings on her walker for feeding to the compost heap when she was done.

Laura sipped her wine, ate one of the buttery cheese straws on which they had both become keen, then thoughtlessly drank the rest of the glass and topped it up. She reflected how lucky they were to have a garden that wasn't overlooked. There was a road to the front and left, the chasm of the railway cutting to the back and their only neighbour was the happy-clappy church, which had high stained glass and no windows that could be peered through, disapprovingly or otherwise.

In Islington her parents had lived in a semi-detached house and, even with high hedges, had been obliged to confine their William and Mrs Blake sessions to a sort of arbour created at its rear with much trellis and a vine so vigorous it was forever bringing sections of the trellis down.

As soon as she was old enough to be coming and going on her own, Dad established a warning code. If he set the milk bottle counter to *No Milk Today* it meant one or both of them had nothing on. The mere thought of this, and the worry of how she would divert or stall visitors to prevent a scandal, was enough to stop her ever inviting people home.

The guaranteed privacy at the Winchester house, quite apart from its Gothic charm, had been a major factor in her mother's impulsive move from Islington. The property had a six-foot wall on all four sides, a typical Hampshire one in which a brick framework was filled with knapped flint cut on the square, and the gate was as high as the wall and had a tiny door at face height that opened on a grilled peephole. There was also a bell pull let into the gatepost. At one end of a long street of expansive villas, most of which had temptingly ungated entrances, it stood, a lone Puritan, impregnable without invitation.

She tired of the radio discussion and, ashamed of cultural cowardice, switched back to the Proms where the piece had either changed or calmed down considerably, then she turned the chops and smeared a little crushed garlic on them. She turned down the heat as Mummy came back in with a bunch of velvety red roses.

'They were being knocked down by the rain,' she said. 'So I thought I'd rescue them. Here. *Etoile de Hollande*. For your bedroom.'

She passed them to Laura and wobbled alarmingly because she hadn't put her walker's brakes on. She was exhilarated by storm and nudity and made Laura feel much the older of them both.

'Thanks,' Laura said. 'They're beautiful,' and she carefully laid the flowers on the draining board so as to pick
up the bath towel and wrap it around her mother's shoulders. 'You're freezing,' she said.

'Nonsense. Warm as toast,' said Mummy, teeth chattering slightly. 'Is that mine?' She pointed at the gin and tonic.

'Yes. Sit and I'll give it to you.'

'What on earth are you listening to?'

'Proms. It's *good* for us.' She helped her mother into
the armchair, wheeled her little invalid's table across her
lap and set gin and cheese straws before her. She was
long past the stage of getting Mummy to wash her hands
before meals if handwashing had not occurred to
Mummy independently.

Over supper they argued. Out of the blue, as she was
finishing her chop, Mummy suddenly said, 'You know,
maybe I should go into a home after all. We could sell
this place to pay the fees, or just let it.'

Laura knew that the heat of her reaction to this was
born of insecurity and the see-sawing of emotions the
offer provoked in her. Of course they could find her a
place in a home and of course they could pay for it by
renting or selling the house but either option would
deprive Laura of a place to live. Possibly she could find
somewhere in the city to rent. On her income she
certainly couldn't afford to buy even a shoebox flat. The
circumstances that had landed the little Parisian bargain
in her lap were not about to be repeated. On the one
hand, Mummy going into a home represented freedom,

on the other, it handed her a fat parcel of guilt. And it would stop them seeing each other so easily.

'Is that honestly what you'd rather?' Laura asked, trying not to sound wounded but suspecting she did. 'Would you really rather be looked after by professional carers and trained moppers-up who you don't know than stay here with me? I mean, it's your house, it's your money, your life but … If I had to move away again, visits from me would be pretty rare.'

Mummy carefully ate the last of her lamb fat and tucked her knife and fork together. 'That never bothered me especially before,' she said.

'Even coming from you, that's pretty cold.'

'It's not coldness,' Mummy retorted. 'It's realism. Anyway. You might settle down at last.'

'Oh, for pity's sake,' Laura shouted.

'You're still young enough to be a stepmother. Don't look at me like that. Stranger things have happened. Some nice rugged divorcee …'

'*Rugged?* Where did that come from?' Laura laughed, and together they escaped into merriment off perilously thin ice.

'You know I *am* rather cold,' Mummy said at last.

'You're not,' Laura assured her, cravenly caving in. 'I didn't mean it.'

'Temperature. Not temperament.'

'Oh. Well, I said you were.'

'Not then. Now. I think it's the draught I was telling you about from the blocked up chimney in here.'

'Not as much flesh to keep you warm as you used to have. Here. Stand up a sec and I'll wrap your dressing gown round you while you eat pudding and I'll start your bath running.'

'Oh, not just yet. It's so early.' She submitted to the dressing gown at least, then confessed, 'Maybe I'm not quite ready for a home.'

'Bedtime at eight in a home. Or earlier, so the staff can get away for the night.'

'Don't!'

Laura laughed. 'They'd change your alarm clock and watch to fool you.'

'*Don't!* Pax.'

Mummy giggled but she looked old and frail again – wisps of hair and pale shoulders catching in the chilly light from under the wall cabinets – a wan shadow suddenly of the majestic Queen Lear who had tended roses in the storm.

HOT DATE

Ben and Bobby slipped through the happy crowd queuing up to enter the back garden of The Bell for Shirley's deferred wake and Ben drove them home. This time he took the town centre route.

'You're a dark horse,' he told Bobby. 'You never told me you were reading.'

'I don't tell you everything.'

'Don't I know it! How's your little problem, by the way?'

'What?'

'You know. Down there. Little friends?'

'Shut up!' Bobby slapped him playfully with the back of a hand.

'No, but really.'

'It's fine. Stuff worked.'

'Good.'

'You're *not* to talk about it!'

191

'I won't. Promise. Forgotten already.'

They crossed the railway bridge and swung right, up Clifton Road. Ben felt Bobby watching him as he drove.

'You're happy,' Bobby said after a while.

'I am.' Ben found them a space at the edge of the Arbour and they walked home from there. The children and terrier had all gone home. Some students were smoking meditatively on the swings. 'Chicken or sausages for supper? There's leftover chicken casserole or –'

'I told you this morning,' Bobby insisted. 'I'm going out. Hot date. Where's your brain today?'

'Don't you want to eat first?'

'Jeff's buying me dinner.'

'He said with maidenly pride.'

'What? Shut up!'

Ben chuckled and let them in. 'When's he getting here?'

'Not for a bit. He's driving the one that gets in at 2015.' Bobby stared at his watch and took a moment to compute the difference between what he saw there and the time Jeff was due. Ben had bought him a watch that showed the twenty-four-hour system around its dial when he took the job at the station to help him with the timetables. 'Shit,' Bobby said shortly and started for the stairs. He turned back. 'If he … If he turns up before I'm ready, be nice.'

'Will do.'

'He's a bit shy, Ben.'

'So am I! Go!'

Bobby thumped up the stairs for what was probably his third shower of the day. Ben hooked his jacket over the back of a chair, turned on the oven, slid in the left-over casserole and some cold baked potatoes then poured himself a glass of yesterday's Rioja and flopped on the sofa.

There was a folder of notes he needed to look over for a lunchtime clinic meeting on Monday. He remembered slinging it down with his things when he came home earlier but Bobby had tidied them away – perhaps to express his impatience when Ben insisted on showering and changing before the service. He'd dig the file out later, tomorrow perhaps. He had all weekend after all. Even if Laura could get away at some point, as he hoped, it seemed unlikely her mother would spare her more than a few hours. Or that her own, clearly power-ful, sense of filial duty would. Perhaps, he reflected, he could see the two of them together again but on a more open footing? He could clean the car and take them out into the surrounding countryside somewhere. He pictured a riverside pub, with ducks and barbecue smoke and Professor Jellicoe falling asleep on the back seat on the way home so that they had to talk in murmurs.

So, rather than hunt for files, he reached for the tele-vision controls and started to watch the news. He had barely watched one story through when the doorbell rang. He flicked the mute button and answered the door. 'You must be Jeff.'

Jeff seemed huge. He wasn't fat, just hefty and big-limbed. He still had on his navy blue train company uniform and was carrying that mysterious black bag train drivers always seemed to have about them. Ben made a mental note, because he had always wondered, to ask Bobby to find out what was in it. Jeff had taken off his jacket and rolled up his sleeves with great neatness, to reveal forearms like a pair of hairy hams. Ben remembered the hairy wrists on last night's visitor and wondered if forearms were Bobby's weakness, the way some men went for breasts or legs, and what had nourished this appetite in a man with no father or uncles to carry him around the room as a child. Ben's own forearms were smooth and he felt effete by comparison.

'You must be Ben,' Jeff said and enveloped Ben's hand in a bear paw. His smile was dazzling against a day's dark growth of stubble. 'Sorry I'm late.'

'You're right on time. It's Bobby who's behind. He's showering in your honour. Have a seat.'

With Jeff safely in an armchair, it felt as though the tiny room had suddenly got its light back.

'Drink?'

'Anything soft? It's still hot out there.'

'Ginger beer?' Ben offered.

'I can live with the pun.'

'Sorry?'

'Yes, please.' While Ben fetched his drink, Jeff chatted on, nervously or out of uncomplicated friendliness. 'I told him not to get all gussied up. It's not fair when I've been stuck in a train all day and not had a chance to … Still. What can you do? We're only going to a pub. I mean, it's a nice pub but it's not a white linen tablecloth job. Oh. Ta.' He took the drink and drank most of it in a single draught. 'Nectar,' he said and gave that twinkly smile again. His charm was wasted in a train cab. It had such presence it made even Ben feel bashful.

'Have you lived in Winchester long?' he asked him.

'I live outside a bit. Edge of Hursley.'

'I know.'

'I was from Gosport originally. Joined the navy straight out of school and left it for the railways ten years ago. Bobby gave me a free cappuccino in his first week at work.'

'Took your time asking him out.'

'Yeah, well, I didn't know he was available.'

They both laughed and Jeff watched the muted news.

'Jeff, speaking as a doctor and his brother …'

'It's okay. I know all about Mosaic Down's Syndrome. He told me in his second week at work.'

'No … I mean, about his heart. You know he has a weak one?'

'I guessed he might, even with the bike riding. I'm a trained first responder. I've got all the kit in my car boot.'

'Oh, well, then I needn't worry.' They both laughed again. 'He's very independent,' Ben went on.

'Tell me about it.'

'But I worry. Since our mum died I …'

Jeff looked back from the news. 'He's in safe hands, Ben.' They exchanged a smile as Bobby left his room in his usual stomping rush but then descended the stairs with a debutante's restraint. He had discarded his suit and tie in favour of jeans and an unflatteringly tight sky-blue tee shirt that said *Fragile* across the chest.

Ben experienced a moment of brotherly panic that the gloriously mismatched pair might snog in front of him but Bobby was discretion itself and, as Jeff rose from his chair and once again seemed to block all the light from the room, he merely said, 'Oh. I didn't hear you arrive. Spared you the baby photos, then. Shall we be off?'

'Sure, Babe,' Jeff muttered and crushed Ben's hand again. 'See you soon,' he said and headed out.

Ben grinned at Bobby.

'What?' Bobby said.

'He's lovely.'

'Well, don't wait up. And don't *worry*.'

'I'm not worrying.'

'Everything's going to be fine. I was a bit naughty, Ben.'

'How do you mean?' Ben remembered Bobby's impish evasiveness before they left for St Cross. All those *nothings*. Bobby was pulling the same expression now. 'What have you done, Bob?'

Bobby had done some terrible things in his time, nearly always in the spirit of being loving and helpful. Machine-washing their mother's one and only piece of cashmere sprang to mind, along with starting to wall-paper the bathroom as a surprise and unplugging a laden freezer just before they went on a three-week summer holiday.

The recollection of such disastrous kindnesses might have started to show on Ben's expression because Bobby's smile dropped a fraction. 'It's okay,' he said. 'It's something nice. I posted your letter, was all.'

Ben didn't understand right away. He tended to neglect domestic admin during the week and was forever getting things like voter registration forms or bank questionnaires into their brown envelopes but neglecting to post them for want of a stamp or sufficient impetus. Chloë had tried, without success, to train him at least to leave all opened mail in one corner of the kitchen. 'I'm sorry?' he said. 'Go on. It doesn't matter and Jeff's waiting out there.'

But Bobby didn't go; he was concerned now in case he'd done something wrong after all. 'The nice letter,' he explained. 'I'd tidied up while you were showering. Because of Jeff coming. It fell out of your case. I guessed you hadn't sent it because you weren't sure. But I'm sure. She loves you, Ben. Of course she does.'

'But you don't have her address,' Ben said, feeling dizzy.

'You daft twat.' He ruffled Ben's hair and walked out. 'You've only been married to her twenty years.' He shut the door behind him and hurried out to where Jeff was thoughtfully refolding his cuffs and the happy pair saun-tered out of sight.

Ben took a while to find the leather portfolio he'd so stupidly left unzipped. Bobby had perched it on a bookshelf under a neatly stacked heap of entirely unrelated papers – takeaway menus, flyers from car valets and window cleaners, a bank statement and a council tax notice and a glossy brochure detailing the many ways in which the council tax was spent.

He tipped the file and papers from the hospital onto the table and forced himself to go through them carefully because the page he was looking for was written in such a happy daze it could have been slotted in at any point. Finally his spirits leapt when he thought he'd found it somewhere at the very back of the file but they fell again when he saw it was one of several rough drafts, unfinished and unsigned.

Clutching at straws, he left the front door carelessly open to run up the street to their nearest letter box. A little notice, blamelessly cruel, informed him the last collection from that box would have been made roughly while they were singing *All Things Bright and Beautiful*. The letter to Laura, brim full of love and apologies and the assurance that, with her agreement, they would now be together for ever, was already on its way to Chloë.

Back in the house he reread the draft, forcing himself to note the various points at which Chloë would quite understandably believe it was addressed to her and no one else. The address not to Laura but to darling, which, like Laura, she had never cared for. The references to her unexpected visit to the clinic, to his recent wounding behaviour … He thought about ringing her, risking her ridicule by telling her not to open it when it came. But who could resist tearing into such an intriguing Pandora's box?

He read the draft again and as he read, he pictured Chloë reading it the following morning. She'd be in the kitchen, luxuriating in its being Saturday. The window would be open onto the tiny balcony where she kept trying to grow herbs. She'd have dressed already, to slip out for the papers and some healthy treat or other for breakfast, but she'd be in comfortable weekend clothes. She wouldn't understand the letter at first and, like everyone, she always had trouble picking through his handwriting. She would have on the tortoiseshell reading glasses she always used around the flat at weekends to give her eyes time off from contact lenses and the steam from her coffee would fog them as she sipped while deciphering. In her attempt to understand, her mouth would be slightly open in the way he used to find sexy when he still thought she was clever. He pictured the way she would reread *I love you and I want to be with you always, whatever it takes and whatever compromises or sacrifices that involves me in*. Would she smile? When she read *all my love, absolutely all of it*, would she cry? Of course not. It was grotesque egotism even to imagine it. But having set it thoughtfully aside to finish her coffee and eat another slice of pineapple, she would pick it up and read it again. And by the time she set it down a second time, phrases from it would have lodged in her heart, and her morning, even, however briefly, her outlook on her life, would be transformed.

Bobby's handwriting was appalling, but he would have used capitals to address the envelope, the way he always did when he knew clarity mattered. He would have taken great care to write the diaeresis of the E of Chloë as two perky little circles, flowers even.

Laura's forgiving visit to the clinic that afternoon had convinced him he had to tell Chloë now, hurt her to set her free, divorce her, leaving her flat and fortune her own. The decision powered the writing of the letter's several drafts, buoyed his sunny walk home and had probably contributed to his teariness in church. But to tell her now, after apparently sending her such a letter (and with his brother's lovable connivance), would be inhumanly cruel. And cruelty, even the indirect cruelty of distance, silence and neglect, was not enough. With a hot wave of shame he recognized afresh that no amount of disdain or mistreatment would drive her away from him because of her dogged conviction, however much feelings between them cooled, that he was a good man whose principles somehow blessed her and cancelled out her father's relative lack of them.

He rang the hotel by the law courts, the one he now thought of as *theirs*, and booked the only room they had left. Then he climbed the stairs and took from the back of his sock drawer an old Roger et Gallet soap box that contained a few things of his mother's and spent a few thoughtful minutes picking through it. Back downstairs he poured himself another glass of wine and drank it very fast, walking from room to tiny room as though the house itself might offer up some merciful alternative to what he had in mind.

Then he poured another and rang Laura.

BATHTIME

As the last of the storm wind stirred about the house, rattling windows and insinuating draughts of humid garden air, Laura padded up the stairs in the wake of the stair-lift, Mummy riding before her, impassively stoical. The scent of the current favourite bubble bath reached them on clouds of steam. It was blue and smelt of water mint with surprising accuracy for something so cheap. She waited as usual for her mother to go in on her own and use the lavatory. The radio being turned on and the door opened would be the signal to join her. Without it being much discussed they had arrived at a routine.

When she first moved in, Laura had found the bathroom one of the most immediately charming rooms in the house: wood-panelled, painted cream, with a low, sloping ceiling and a deepset casement window that afforded one a view of trees from the lavatory but complete privacy. It looked out across the railway cutting so the pleasure of lying in the bath was enhanced by the roar of a passing train down below the trees and the thought of all those passengers still hours from such a soothing.

After the breaking of Mummy's hip and ankle and the onset of her tendency to fall, the room had come to reveal its unsuitability. Ugly grab rails and handles had been fixed on every side by a man from the council's disability support unit and a care worker had equipped the lavatory with a freestanding support frame, like a titanic metal clothes horse, and a plastic extension unit, which had raised its perching height by nearly a foot.

These ugly additions were part of the price of precious independence but they brought with them a grim whiff of the care home Laura had hoped to avoid and a no less lowering sense of entering a narrowing one-way street to debility. As did the commode.

The *commode*. The very word, with its lip-puckering French gentility, stood in opposition to everything her mother cherished, and its ugly design – it was a turquoise plastic throne with a wirehandled half-bucket in its middle, coyly concealed by what looked like a plastic dustbin lid – would have fitted in no better among their old Ripplevale Grove furniture than it did with the Jellicoe family treasures. The commode had been dropped off by their care worker after a couple of distressing incidents where Mummy had failed to hobble to the bathroom in time when she woke in the night. And, like all the handles in the bathroom and the electric lift which now ruled the stairs, it silently asserted itself as a fixture-unto-death.

At the moment Laura could manage bath times on her own but at some point they would have to rip out the bath and install a walk-in model or a shower. The room was far too small to allow for both a shower and a bath. She had already investigated, with the help of the inexhaustibly patient woman at Age Concern, and found a shower model with a sturdy slatted bench that folded down from the wall and not too high a pedestal edge to the base – so that even a bather barely able to lift their legs could step inside. The subject had been raised and swatted aside a few times. Mummy was not keen. She was convinced all showers soaked one's hair unavoidably and she hated washing her hair more than twice a week. But at least Laura had the facts at her disposal and sometimes, she had discovered, the early raising of an unpalatable topic served as a kind of vaccination against the time when it would need to be raised in earnest.

While she waited for her summons, Laura carried the bundle of discarded clothes into her mother's room, hung up the dress to dry and set aside the fortified underwear, which for once had seen almost a full day's wear, for adding to the small load she would set to wash overnight.

She had not been so well acquainted with her mother's wardrobe since childhood. Then, she had raided it to try on hats and shoes and to gaze in wonder at the complexities of bras and suspender belts. Perhaps precisely because she had lived as a naturist, Mummy had always dressed well on her tight budget, and precisely because her naked body held no mystery for Laura, the clothes she chose to dress it in and the mysteries of how they came together to good effect had a heightened fascination for her. When clothes were not a given, they counted more.

She turned on the bedside light – a very pretty wooden one she coveted, carved to resemble a segmented palm trunk – turned down the bed, pulled tight the sheet rumpled by her mother's afternoon nap then turned off the overhead light. She might have raised no children of her own but she remembered her own girlhood strongly enough to know that these evening scenes carried echoes of a child's bedtime. She couldn't decide, however, if that was disturbing or a source of reassurance. To scrub a parent's back for them and wash their hair without getting soap in their eyes, to furl them in a fluffy bath towel and see them safely into a warm and comfortable bed and still their fretting about the night and day to come was a chance to demonstrate love in circumstances where words did not come easily.

And yet. Oh, and yet.

There was a frightening meekness in her mother sometimes now, something horrifying about the ease with which a woman so witheringly self-possessed in other areas had ceded her right to privacy in this. Summer clothes were easily shed but winter layers, especially tights and vests, needed assistance. One had only to say *skin a rabbit* for her arms to point up in childish eagerness for the drawing off of vest or jersey.

The bathroom door opened and through it, along with a renewed gust of scented steam, came the applause for the end of that evening's Prom.

'Coming,' Laura called, drew the curtains to block out the glow of a streetlamp which Mummy said kept her awake and crossed the landing.

She needed help getting her legs over the side of the bath, that was all. They had an electric device called the Tritoness. It was a large, sea-green cushion of some rubbery material which, when fully inflated by a little motor, reached to the top of the bath. Mummy sat on the flat surface at the bath's rear on a plastic carrier bag, Laura gently manoeuvred her legs up and swivelled her on the bag until her legs were in the bath. She then edged herself forwards onto the Tritoness, whose motor would release air from it until she was sitting on the bath's bottom. Bathing done, the same motor pumped air back in and the Tritoness raised her, like Venus from the waves, as she felt prompted to murmur most nights.

Only Mummy had become convinced she couldn't make the Tritoness work on her own. All she had to do was press a button. Perhaps she was scared of electrocution – although the control panel was designed to be safely used by wet fingers and was sealed behind a waterproof layer for extra security. Anyway, for whatever reason, she insisted that only Laura – *Clever Laura* she became at this moment – could make the device work. Having been lowered in, there was no reason she shouldn't be left to enjoy the radio and the bath and

Laura had tried leaving her to wash herself but she only became fretful if she had to call out to be helped with anything. And recently some childlike impulse of vulnerability, or loneliness even, always prompted her to keep Laura there with little bursts of conversation until she was ready to emerge.

Apart from her hair, which Laura washed because Mummy was apt to neglect it if she didn't, and her back, which rheumatic shoulders no longer let her reach, she still washed herself, rubbing all the bits she could reach with a flannel. She couldn't reach her feet any more but she wouldn't let Laura touch them either as she claimed her fingernails tickled. Instead, on the recommendation of the chiropodist who called by every other Monday to file her heels and cut her toenails, she had acquired off the Internet a device like a giant plastic nail brush – she dubbed it the *Pixy's Doormat* – which attached near the plughole with a series of suction pads. Laura had taken to using it too, dreamily rubbing her feet on it when it was her turn, as the sensation was unexpectedly delicious.

She could tell Mummy was using it now because she couldn't seem to use it and talk at the same time. Her conversation dried up and she stared at the ceiling, wearing a thoughtful expression like a toddler's while filling its nappy. Did one feel desire at eighty? Was her mother's eye still snagged by male beauty, by this man's meaty legs or the curls on that one's nape, or was the restless hunger finally switched off? Perhaps lust transmuted at last into easy pleasures like wiping one's feet on the *Pixy's Door-mat* or having someone rub one's scalp while washing one's hair. For lust to continue when the body that housed it was giving out would be too unkind to be borne, but it was not a query one could put to one's mother.

'Would you mind doing the honours?' Mummy asked, focused again, and Laura bent forward to pull out the plug then click the Tritoness into action. It began its chuntering sounds, air pipe vibrating, and the balloon slowly reinflated, lifting Mummy as Laura stood ready with a warm towel held before her.

'Venus from the waves,' sighed Mummy.

MINIBAR SNACKS

They had been allocated the room directly above the one they had always had before. At first it seemed almost identical: same floor plan, same bed, same furniture and curtains. Then he noticed the ceiling was lower, and the windows smaller and the pictures different and he saw there was only a shower where the other afforded a luxurious, claw footed bath. Of course it was only an accident but it felt to Ben like an insidious draining down of expectation.

He came there almost at once, even though he knew she could not possibly get away without notice like this until her mother was in bed, because simply sitting at home watching the clock would have been beyond him. But waiting in a hotel room proved little better. Everything about it suggested self-indulgence – albeit on a lesser scale than their old room – and could not have chimed less well with his mood. A soulless motel just off the M3 with a bar haunted by sales reps might have been more apt or a sordid room over a pub, the sort where one collected a key from an ask-no-questions landlord. He doubted Winchester offered either these days, if indeed it ever had.

At least it was dark at last so he felt he could draw the heavy curtains without it seeming odd. He kicked off his shoes and tried lying on the bed. Then he tried sitting up in the solitary, button-backed armchair but that proved toughly ornamental. Nerves had stopped him touching the casserole he had reheated but now that smells from the restaurant were reaching him he was seized with an inappropriate hunger. He ate the packet of crisps from the mini-bar. Then the nuts. Then he felt ashamed and hid the wrappers far under the bed in case she saw them and thought him insensitive.

Finally she rang him on his mobile to say she was on her way.

He bit his tongue to stop himself calling her *darling* in his nervousness. 'It's room eleven,' he said. He knew she'd rather come straight up than face the fluster of dealing with a receptionist. But then he couldn't bear to wait in the room a moment longer and he hurried downstairs to watch for her from the hotel steps.

The noise from the restaurant and bar's open windows behind him, moneyed, Friday-nightish, made him feel peculiarly self-conscious and alone so he waved when he saw her emerge from the leafy short cut she liked to take across the old Green Jackets' barracks.

She waved back and he was so happy to see her again so soon that he almost forgot why he was there. Every time he saw her was a kind of reminder. It wasn't that he forgot how she looked in between meetings but that his thoughts of her were so intertwined now with his memories of her younger self. Her every reappearance before him was a reminder that she was self-assured now, purposeful and debonair. To see her was to remember how much of her adult life was still hidden from him. Tonight she had on an ethnic necklace he had admired on her before, outsized silver beads which jangled against her as she broke into a run to join him. She seized his hand and kissed it. He drew her to him and kissed her forehead. Her hair smelled of lavender. And fried onions. 'You always smell so good,' he said.

'That'll be the supper I cooked earlier. Someone was saying the other day how wearing scent to attract a man is a waste of time and what women should really do is fry bacon just before leaving the house.'

He kissed her again and playfully sniffed her hair. 'Sorry,' he said. 'I couldn't stand it in the room on my own.'

'Let's see if it's better with two of us.'

'Let's.'

She drew him in after her and said a lively hello to the young man on reception duty.

'We've already checked in,' Ben told him and hurried up the stairs after her. She had changed out of the dress she had on earlier. She wore black trousers made of some kind of linen and a very simple, tailored white shirt, untucked, through which he could see the outline of her bra as she climbed ahead of him.

'Room twelve, isn't it?' she called, starting to open the wrong door.

'Eleven,' he hissed. 'Here!' and she ran back to him, giggling.

They made love, of course. How could they not? Although it felt to him like a kind of treachery when he had planned to be gravely respectful. They both became wildly overheated, amidst all the bedding and drapes, and at one point she sprang panting away from him and dragged back all the curtains and threw up the little windows so that they ended with the noise and lights of Southgate Street all about them and it was almost like having the bed out on a balcony. Then they raided the mini-bar and started to kiss again.

'I wrote to you,' he admitted. 'I wrote you several drafts and even made a fair copy in my very best doctor's handwriting.'

'Oh yes?'

He could hear she was smiling in anticipation but he realized he couldn't possibly tell her where the letter had gone.

'So what did you write?' she asked. She had taken off her heavy Moroccan beads finally because they were bothering her but was amusing herself by rubbing their silvery ridges along his thigh. In the flickering lights from outside she looked thirty or younger, her eyes dark and glistening. He reached out to turn the bedside lamp on but she stayed his hand. 'Please,' she said. 'Not yet.'

'I wrote that I loved you,' he said. 'I said I realized I always had. That I hoped you could forgive me for having been such an idiot and hurt you so.'

'Ssh,' she said. 'How can you ask? It's the past now.'

'It matters.'

He saw her smile, or rather, he heard the little outrush of breath and saw the glisten of her teeth. 'You're such a *boy* sometimes,' she said. 'This is all that matters. Us. Here and now.'

'You never told me who your mother was.'

'Why should I have? She was just my mother.'

'Yes, but ...' He wondered how to continue. The temptation to break off was intense. 'I had met her before, you know. Years ago. At Oxford. In our last year. She knew the warden or someone there.'

'Did you really meet her? We led very separate lives then. She came up for work things quite often but I didn't encourage her to contact me. I was too wrapped up in the selfish pleasures of being a student to want her ticking me off or cutting me down to size in front of my friends. She won't remember. She met hundreds of students a year, probably.'

'Why didn't you boast about her?'

'She wasn't exactly cool, even then. Especially then.'

And he saw that it would be monstrous to tell her of her mother's entirely innocent role in the unlacing of

219

their love. That particular vial of poison was to be his alone.

'I'm afraid,' Laura went on, mockingly, 'you probably made a much smaller impression on her than she did on you. She liked you as a grown-up, though. The other day. You must have pressed the virology button when I wasn't listening.'

'Really?'

'Her G spot, socially. A man could have all the charm of Goebbels but if he murmured *Porcine Circovirus* or *Lymphocytic Choriomeningitis*, she'd bat her eyelashes and move a little closer. It's amazing, really, that my dad even got as far as a first date.' She laughed to herself. 'Poor Dad. He was such a saint, really.'

He took the hand that was holding the beads and clutched it to his lips to draw her attention back. 'Laura?' he told her. 'I've got to go home.'

'Bobby?'

'No. Battersea home. Back to the fucking flat and ... back to Chloë. I've got to deal with her and stop being such a coward. It's not fair to either of you.'

'So it isn't all over.'

'It *is*.' And maybe it was, he told himself. 'It is in my head but I've got to bring it home to her. You saw her the other day.'

'She still loves you.'

'God. Maybe. I suppose. She's ... She's not very bright and she's extremely ... She's used to being loved. Her father ...'

220

She cut him off. 'You'll be back soon, though. Next week. The hospital.'

'I don't know,' he said. 'I expect so. Hope so. If I don't handle it right she'll make our lives hell, though. I might grab a few days' leave so I can do it right.'

'Oh.'

She pulled the sheet up and withdrew slightly, watching him. Now he turned the bedside light on.

'Please, no,' she said.

'I've got to,' he said. 'Just for a second or two. Here. I'll dim it.'

He extricated himself from the tangle of sheets and went over to where his trousers had ended up, deep in the slithery mound of tossed aside damask cushions and quilted bedspread. He reached into the pocket for the little jeweller's box and climbed back on the bed. 'Here,' he said.

He took her hand, slipped the box into her palm and pressed them both against his heart because he couldn't speak and was afraid of crying. She had never seen him weep.

'What is it?' she said, frowning slightly. 'God, Ben, what?' She withdrew her hand and looked at the box and opened it. 'Ben?'

'It probably doesn't fit.'

'It's lovely.'

'And it's probably fifty years' bad luck because he walked out on her.'

'Your mum's engagement ring?'

221

'Yes. Will you …? Does it fit?'

She slipped it onto her ring finger. She looked at it in the light, smiled at him. 'My hands are sturdier than you imagine,' she said. 'It's really lovely, Ben.' She sniffed and dabbed away a tear with a fistful of sheet. 'Silly,' she told herself. 'Sorry. I wish I'd met her.'

'I wish she'd met you. I should have brought you home the very first Christmas. What were we thinking of staying in that freezing house in Oxford?'

'We were trying to be grown up. Playing house.'

He took her hand again to look at the ring on it. He worried it might look mean. He knew nothing about jewellery. It had never occurred to him until now that his father's taste might have been suspect. 'I mean, I can't ask you,' he said. 'I'm not free to ask you properly. Not yet.'

'I know.'

'But can I ask you to, well, sort of wait?'

She looked him full in the face and it was a kind of promise mixed with challenge. 'Of course,' she said.

'Good.'

'I'm going nowhere.'

'Good.'

'What about your brother?'

'Oh … I can't pretend Bobby needs me nearly as much as I'd convinced myself he did. Bobby'll be just fine. He'll be glad to get shot of me. He might even have the love of a good man. As soon as I get back I want you two to meet.'

'That'll be nice.'

She clung to him for a minute or two then kissed his shoulder abruptly and got up. 'I must get back,' she said. 'I told her I was going for a walk. Even though she was half-asleep when I left, she'll start to worry if I don't come back. There are always drunken students in the streets around us on a Friday and she'll be on edge with the noise.'

'I'll walk you back.'

'No need.'

But he did. She waited out on the pavement while he quickly paid for the room then they walked arm in arm up the dark little passage beside the hotel garden, around the back of Searle's House and through the odd mixture of converted barracks buildings and incongruous, slightly Toytown housing that had been thrown up since the regiment moved out. He won a little extra time by persuading her into a diversion up to the old parade ground where regimented lavender bushes and conifers now stood in for companies on parade and a curiously desolate fountain was playing vigorously in the middle of a large, round pond. He told her how he remembered lying in bed on summer nights as a small boy, hearing the marching band practising there. They happened to be passing the pond as the automated system switched off the flow for the night so the last jet of water fell beside them with a distinctly unromantic noise, like the emptying of a slops bucket.

'Wish,' he told her, squeezing her arm, but she ran a tidying hand through her hair and sighed.

'Oh. Me? I'm all wished out.'

'Hope, then.'

'Hmm,' she said and he wished he'd had the self-possession to hold his tongue.

They followed a path off the parade ground through a narrow arch in one of the new buildings thrown up to echo the old, and down a flight of steps and all too suddenly were on St James Lane and just across the road from her mother's house.

'When are you off?' she asked.

'Tomorrow,' he said. 'Best to seize the nettle over the weekend.'

'I hate goodbyes,' she admitted. 'I'm rubbish at them.'

'So don't bother. Who knows, I might be back on Sunday or even tomorrow night. We can speak.'

It was as though he wanted to raise his spirits as much as hers but she wouldn't be drawn. She raised the hand with his mother's ring on it and touched the side of his face. 'Bye, Beautiful,' she said and slipped across the road before he could catch her or hold her or even think of anything to say back. She let herself in through the gate and was lost to view.

He walked a short way down the hill until he was far enough away to glimpse the little Gothic windows on the house's first floor. One of them was already lit so perhaps Professor Jellicoe had stayed up reading or simply fallen asleep over her book. He imagined Laura going in to her and gently slipping a copy of *Haemorrhagic Fever and Primate Lesions* out of her grasp before turning out the light.

But the light stayed on so perhaps her mother was still awake and asking after her walk or calling out for a nightcap or painkillers. And then, at last, the second window lit up and he had a fleeting glimpse of her, through a tangle of rose branches, reaching up to tug the curtains across. He knew, because she had confided her habit to him, that if he waited long enough he would see her light go out and her hands drawing the curtains back again because she liked to wake to the sunlight rather than to an alarm. But he sensed that would have been creepy of him.

Rather than head for home across the barracks and have to pass the desolate pool again, he climbed the hill a little further, crossing the railway bridge, and walked back along St James Terrace, a row of prettily gardened houses that faced the barracks across a pedestrian path and the railway cutting. A late express flew by beneath as he walked, heading for the coast. He looked down into the cutting to see its lit up, seemingly empty carriages flashing by far below and its retreating sound seemed suddenly to name his despair.

It did not occur to him until he woke the following morning, at dawn but still far too late for it to be of any use, that he could have driven up to London immediately after leaving her, driven up, lain in wait in the car and let himself into the hall just before the postman. Or even waylaid the postman on the doorstep with a cheerful greeting and an offer to carry the letters in for him.

Advance strategy had never been his strong point.

NIGHTCAP

Between putting Mummy to bed and going to bed herself had become what Laura thought of as her time. Even though she was often exhausted and ready for an early night herself, it felt important to do something that had nothing to do with her mother, if only to admit defeat after half an hour. She could download and answer e-mails, read a book or watch television; she was addicted to violent police forensics dramas Mummy abhorred and would have talked through. But what she usually did was the one thing her mother could no longer do: take a walk. She liked walking. She used to walk the pavements of the Marais for hours, especially at night. It was something she missed. And it was good to get out and see some life.

Not that there was much of this on Winchester's residential streets at nine forty-five on a Friday. She might meet a smattering of noisy students, a few impatient dog walkers, the occasional late commuter walking from the station. But it was a city where people were slow to draw their curtains at night, especially in the summer when darkness stole on slyly, and after nearly two years of living there she had yet to grow blasé about the intimate visions this offered. Domestic lives in central Paris were hidden from view in apartments high above pavement level and even so were tucked behind shutters. And she had retained her Parisian insouciance about staring.

Tonight she felt more than usually restless and the storm had created a freshness and promise in the night, so she walked further than usual. She walked down the hill to Southgate Street then cut through the network of sporadically lit side streets towards the floodlit cathedral that seemed to float above the houses like a great ghostly boat.

Walking past mothy, scented gardens like the one she had left at home, she stared in at families talking over wreckages of meals, at wordless, slumped couples lit by television, at a woman intently reading in an armchair. She surprised a man and woman who had slipped out from a noisy dinner party to smoke and flirt and sensed from their hostile stares that she had been watching them with a kind of hunger, and moved hastily on.

Then she stood for a few minutes looking up from Great Minster Street at the cathedral's west end, near where she knew there was a funny-sad tombstone for a militiaman who had died from drinking too much cold small beer. She walked on, between some busy pubs, past the Butter Cross and up the high street. She climbed the hill at a brisk pace, relishing the exercise to her calves, past the law courts and Great Hall. Her intention had been to cut left through the old barracks for home but an impulse led her on, over the railway bridge and to the right, across the deserted reaches of Oram's Arbour.

She had done this several times: gone to stand outside the house in Fulflood where Ben had taken her occasionally. She was careful not to do it so often as to make it a ritual but she was aware there was a ritualistic element to the excursion; she needed to see the little house, remind herself it was real and, of course, reassure herself he wasn't there.

Bobby was still there. He still didn't know who she was, naturally, as they'd never been introduced, but she had seen him walking around the house occasionally, sometimes alone, sometimes with his big friend. The first time she had seen him in the house she immediately recognized him as the man from the station newsagents and thereafter she made a point of buying something from him whenever she was passing through to visit clients or friends in London. She would buy a paper from him, or a paper and a coffee as well, so as to have a chance to exchange a few words. She never said much more than, 'Chilly today, isn't it?' or 'Maybe I'll be a devil and have one of those flapjacks too,' or 'What an elegant tie!' and he said little back and probably didn't remember her from one exchange to the next, but he was always pleasant and she had come to feel that keeping an eye on him was somehow important. Had he not been in the shop or had she come to the house and found it empty and up for sale suddenly, something small but crucial in her would have died on the spot.

Bobby was there tonight. He and his big friend were on the sofa in the tiny living room watching television. She could hear the programme noise through their open window, a girl band singing, she decided. They had made some changes recently. The windows and door had been repainted. The little patch between the front of the house and the pavement railings had been carefully filled with very clean gravel and there was lavender growing in pots there, and a little clipped bay tree. They had acquired a cat, too, which startled her by suddenly banging out through the cat flap they had cut in the front door.

All was well. Reassured, she walked back along the top of the Arbour, down the hill and home along St James Terrace.

The temperature was rising again and walking had made her warm. She hoped another storm wasn't brewing. As she let herself in at the gate with a practised lack of clatter, she glanced up and saw her mother's window was dark.

The wine with supper had been rather good. She pulled out the rubber stopper and poured herself another glass of it then carried that and a couple of cheese straws back into the garden along with a cushion. She sat in her mother's usual chair, the most comfortable one, kicked off her shoes and stretched out her legs. She sipped her wine, munched a biscuit and lay back staring at where the stars would be if only someone would turn the streetlamps off. There was a song thrush that regularly mistook the nearest lamp for the onset of dawn and would sing as strongly and sweetly as any nightingale, but tonight, so far, he was silent.

Ben had been gone exactly a year to the week and she had heard nothing. Not a call, not a letter.

She had decided, the morning after they said goodbye, that she would not contact him but would give him all the time he needed. Then, as the days passed and she still heard nothing, she tried ringing him at the hospital and was told he no longer worked there. Fired up by that, she rang the Chelsea and Westminster and waited long enough for the receptionist to say, 'Putting you through now,' before she hung up.

She still had his mobile number stored on her mobile of course. As days turned to weeks, she felt more and more tempted to ring it. She thought about ringing then hanging up at once so that her name would appear, pang-inducingly, in his missed calls log. She thought about simply texting him a question mark.

Then, when she had drunk too much over supper one night and realized she was highly likely to ring him and cry or say something demeaning to either or both of them, she deleted his number from her telephone. She regretted this of course, doubly so in the sobriety of morning. She could still have reached him through work but that would have seemed forlorn somehow, or underhand, like the behaviour of a stalker or someone jilted.

And she did not feel jilted, even one year on. Ben was weak or, fatal combination, weak and good. Jilting implied, if not malice, then aforethought and he was considerate to a fault and not a planner. As he had confessed all those months ago in the restaurant, he was not the powerful one in his marriage, not when Chloë was near enough to influence him.

As the weeks wore on Laura realized that whatever offstage battle had taken place, she had lost. Chloë might not love him more, but her love, it seemed, had proved the most tenacious. And, who knew, perhaps she had surprised them both with her strength of feeling. Perhaps it had taken such a crisis for him finally to fall in love with her and he had woken to the novel wonder of her as a man returning from a fever would be astounded at the mundane pleasure of grapes or daisies.

Laura owned no photographs of him, not even old ones, and her mental ones were already so fuzzy about the edges that, in dreams, his manly self became disturbingly conflated with the boyish version she seemed to remember more distinctly. Awake, she often thought of his mouth and chin, in close-up; the fetching little gap between his front teeth. But always, loving as she did like a blind woman, it was his voice and his scent that came first when she thought of him.

The glimpse she had caught of Chloë at the hospital, however, had etched itself onto her memory and showed no signs of fading.

It had been a shock because Chloë had aged, of course. Without him at her side to make a terrible sense of the moment, Laura would not have recognized her. The coltish blonde in the perfect, wafty frocks, her nemesis from her miserable last weeks at Oxford, had become a woman, with womanly, even childbearing, hips, and less Botticelli hair, dyed a few shades darker and pushed off her face with an Alice band. But what had upset Laura so was seeing that Chloë, Mrs Ben Patterson, who had driven all the way from London bearing her sadly exquisite little birthday cake, had looked kind, and loving and pained. Here was a wife whose husband was having some kind of breakdown or going off the rails but who was prepared to wait for, forgive and even rescue him should the need arise.

As a student, Chloë had maddened girls and melted boys because she was too rich to feel privileged and too pretty to care. Like the fictitious girl of an advertiser's vision, she seemed to have an infinity of alluring possibilities open to her. As an adult, it seemed, those possibilities had evaporated in the heat of love, all her potential had been invested in someone beside herself.

That new image of her had quite eclipsed the old one of her younger self in insouciant triumph. In her troubled hours, Laura summoned it up and found it commanded more respect than resentment. When she pictured that eloquent, wordless little scene in the hospital car park, Ben was now no more than a manly prop, a handsome enough figure in a well-cut suit, but one with his back to the audience. The compassionate focus was all on Chloë. In the instant when she tried to kiss his lips and he moved his face so that she only kissed his brow, she shut her lovely eyes in pain.

Laura took off the ring and set it on the ground beside her, beneath one of the pots of lilies. Then she scrabbled with her fingers and pulled aside a good fistful or more of gravel, pushed the ring into the hole she had made and buried it. She stood, nose freshly filled with the lilies' scent, took another sip of her wine and set the glass down on a little table.

Her cotton dress slipped off easily and she draped it over the table beside the glass. She stood there in her underwear for a minute, getting used to the idea, to the oddly pleasing conjunction of hearing occasional voices or car noise from the road beyond the wall with the tingly sensation of night air on her bare skin. She felt gooseflesh rise on her thighs and arms and her scalp stir in anticipation then she unhooked her bra and scooped off her pants as well.

She walked a little, slowly, wary of the possibility of snails under bare feet, over to the summerhouse and back, towards the house and back. It felt good. She had forgotten how good. She felt as intensely alive as her mother had looked earlier, coming in from the rain. She tried sitting in the chair again, the way she so often saw her mother do, a woman in a garden chair who just happened to have nothing on. It was, perhaps, a little colder than was comfortable. She was unlikely to stay there for long.

Impulsively she drank the rest of her wine then stood abruptly and scrabbled in the gravel beneath the lily pot for some minutes until she had retrieved the ring. She rinsed it in the birdbath nearby and slipped it back on her finger. In only a year, the skin around it had formed a calloused ridge there so that the ring slipping back into place seemed to complete her.

Some students were coming up the hill, boys, singing the *Match of the Day* theme and laughing as they kicked a beer can back and forth. Startled, Laura snatched up her clothes and shoes and hurried inside.

AUTHOR'S NOTE

I owe a huge debt to my mother and sister, who live in Winchester but otherwise in no way resemble the mother and daughter in this book, for their forbearance in letting me draw inspiration both from their relationship of mutual support and from the vigour with which my mother has met the challenges osteoporosis has thrown at her. A novelist in the family is rarely a reassuring thing but they bear me with fortitude …

Thanks are due to Dr Simon Worrell for his generous assistance in so patiently guiding me through a clinical venereologist's daily routine and to Rose in Bideford for her lovely reminiscences of family naturist holidays.

Thanks, too, to my second family – my book family – to Caradoc King, Patricia Parkin and Clare Reihill, for their judicious advice and loving support.

Sainsbury's
Book club
Try something new today

sainsburys.co.uk/bookclub

Sainsbury's Book club

Q & A with Patrick Gale

What inspired you to start writing?
Reading, undoubtedly. I was blessed in coming from the sort of family where everyone read at meals and nobody ever told you off for preferring reading to being sociable. Writing emerged quite naturally from all the reading when I was still quite small and again I was lucky in that I was encouraged but not too much so that I didn't get self-conscious about it. I never thought it would become a career, though. I was trying to become an actor and writing was just something I did, a sort of itch to self-express...

How did you come up with the idea of rekindling a lost love in *The Whole Day Through?*
Initially I'd planned this as a novel about persuasion. Drawing on an experience of my own when I was a student and so profoundly lacking in self-esteem that I let my stronger-willed friends persuade me out of a relationship that could have become something very special, I set out to have Laura persuaded out of the relationship with Ben. Her bossy friend, Amber, would have remained a friend of sorts in adulthood and it would have been a novel as much about friendship as about love. But I think Professor Jellicoe changed all that. As I was developing the novel, she became stronger and stronger and I suddenly had the horrible idea that she might, albeit unwittingly, have stamped on

her daughter's chance of happiness twenty years ago. There's nothing quite like lost love re-found or the still attractive ex stumbled upon unexpectedly. It's so potent because the former lover already knows you and the relationship can resume with such dramatic speed. And then it's only human to wonder, 'Did I make the right choice?' 'How would he have turned out?' No wonder that school reunion websites have proved disastrous for so many marriages!

Even though you often present unusual family set-ups in your novels, and show the power of overwhelming sexual desire, you seem to uphold marriage and commitment too. Do you have a strong conventional side?

Oh heavens, yes. Like a lot of keen gardeners, I suspect that I'm a spiritual Tory, for all that I've read the *Guardian* all my life. I come from an immensely rooted and conventional background. My father's family lived in the house they built for five hundred years and the three generations ending in my grandfather were priests. My father could so nearly have been one too. Both my parents were deeply, privately Christian and had a daunting sense of duty. I rebelled against all this for all of five years in my late teens and early twenties but deep down all I ever wanted to do was move to the country, marry a good upstanding chap and create a garden ... ▶

❛ It's only human to wonder, "Did I make the right choice?" "How would he have turned out?" No wonder that school reunion websites have proved disastrous for so many marriages! ❜

Q & A with Patrick Gale *(continued)*

◄ **Who is your favourite character in the book?**

I'm pretty fond of Ben, actually. I started out worrying he was just going to irritate me by being so hopeless and damaging people by trying to be good. But then precisely that hopelessness of his made me love him. I particularly loved the way his relationship with Bobby developed and the way he'd unwittingly become a way for his brother to discover the pleasure he took in living with another bloke. I suspect at least one of his male nurses is deeply devoted to him and he has no idea...

But I suspect that Laura's worldview and experience is closest to my own. I'm not an accountant – although I do my own book-keeping and VAT returns – but I do have something of her way of standing back from life and, dare I admit, sometimes forgetting to live it.

The depiction of Professor Jellicoe is strong and complex and far from the usual image of a disabled old lady. Who or what inspired you to write about old age and disability in this way?

I've always been impatient with the idea that old age confers sweetness and, thanks to numerous colourful examples in the family when I was growing up, I've always been rather in love with old women so I think it was only a matter of time before I placed one so centrally in a novel. In some ways she's inspired by my mother, who is still alive but maddeningly confined to an old people's home now because of

6 I do have something of [Laura's] way of standing back from life and, dare I admit, sometimes forgetting to live it 9

osteoporosis. It has been so infuriating seeing her life curtailed through something as basic as not being able to climb stairs or step in and out of a shower unassisted when I can feel her mind still surging away. In a way Harriet Jellicoe is an extreme version of something most adult children of ageing parents experience – that sense of a lively mind trapped in a failing body. In Harriet's case I wanted to convey the sense that her mind has always been the most important thing, to the point where she's been prepared to sacrifice everything to it.

Both Ben and Laura look after members of their family in different ways. What is your view on the position of carers in our society today?
Without unpaid carers, Western society would implode within a week. I'm not just thinking of all the adults who care for their parents but of all the children who do so too, often when they're still at school age, and of all the grandparents without whom so many mothers couldn't work to support their families. My mother was ill a lot when we were growing up so I had an early education in the unfair way these situations can arise and take over a family. I was adamant, though, that I wanted to show love, not resentment – or not *just* resentment – in Laura and Ben's caring. It is wonderful to be given the chance to care for a loved one. What's awful is having that caring taken for granted and given no outside support or relief. ▶

6 How I love gardening. I can read seed catalogues in bed 9

Q & A with Patrick Gale *(continued)*

◄ **The power of nature is an important theme in this novel. Do you enjoy gardening?**

How I love gardening. I can read seed catalogues in bed and give a plain man a second glance if he knows his botanical Latin. It's one of the few things I resent about having to travel to promote my work at book festivals – knowing how my garden in Cornwall may be neglected in my absence, how the salad seedlings will have no one to protect them. I'm a great one for smuggling home seeds in my socks from faraway lands to see if I can make them grow.

If I weren't a novelist and couldn't be a psychotherapist (the job I'd do if I had to stop writing), I can imagine being very happy as a jobbing gardener. Nothing fancy, just mowing lawns and pruning rose bushes. Farmer's spouse is a pretty wonderful position too, though. We have a herd of beef cattle and I love working with them.

When and where do you write?

I'm a daylight writer and tend to keep the same writing hours as my husband does farming ones. We get up early and, if I've a book on the go, I'll start writing as soon as I've walked the dogs. In good weather the dog walk often becomes the writing session as I like writing outside and we have a lot of inspiring corners where I can settle, looking out to sea or hunkered in the long grass. We have very patient dogs...

**It is less common now to find a
contemporary novel with a character
dying from an AIDS-related illness.
Did you have any political agenda in
depicting Shirley's death and funeral?**
Not really, but I wanted to remind people
gently that HIV hasn't gone away and
suddenly become this third-world disease.
There are a lot of HIV-positive people
passing you on the street every day. Most
of them are now able to live with HIV,
thanks to amazing advances in drug
development, but there are still the less
fortunate ones and surging STD figures in
the under-twenty-fives illustrate that we
can't afford to be complacent.

**I am interested by the fact that it comes
across as less significant that Bobby is
gay than that he has Down's Syndrome
and a sex life. Why do you think there is
a taboo around this issue?**
As I have Ben observe in the book, people
whose children have Down's Syndrome are
often reluctant to admit that their children
are growing up and developing sexualities.
I think we're really queasy about exploring
the issues this raises, partly because adults
of limited intelligence could so easily fall
victim to abusive relationships but also, I
suspect, from a deep-set reluctance to see
them become something other than an
object of pity who will make us feel better
for pitying them. People with Down's
Syndrome are all too often described as
sweet in just the same patronising way the
old can be. I had to dig pretty deep in my ▶

6 There are gay
and lesbian
people out there
with Down's
Syndrome, of
course there are,
and they're as
out and proud as
the rest of us 9

Q & A with Patrick Gale (*continued*)

◄ research but there are gay and lesbian people out there with Down's Syndrome, of course there are, and they're as out and proud as the rest of us.

I love the structure of the book as it moves through the different stages of one day. Why did you use this form?
I hoped to achieve a sense of gentle inevitability, with the progression of a long soft June day from dawn to nightfall. Once the reader realises, 'Ah, so that's why it's called that and that's the way the story is going,' I could then surprise them with how much I can pack into that day. And, of course, one way of packing it in is with memories. I'm fascinated by the way memories work and in several of my recent novels, notably *Rough Music* and *Notes from an Exhibition*, I've been trying different methods of suggesting the way just thinking about one memory can release another, and even seeing if it's possible to let that memory-darting dictate the structure of an emerging novel.

I found the book to have a very moving, almost elegiac tone at times – perhaps because there is so much loss in the novel: lost love, lost health and lost opportunity. Did you find it an emotional book to write? Did you enjoy writing it?
I loved writing it. I was startled at how short it ended up being but then I realised that some of my favourite books about relationships are short, so I relaxed and set about polishing and polishing the little

❛ I hadn't really mapped how Ben and Laura's story was going to end ❜

thing I'd made rather than fretting it wasn't some *magnum opus*. I was terribly upset when I realised how sad it was going to become – not just about love but ageing and death and, well, human fragility – as I hadn't planned that. I hadn't really mapped how Ben and Laura's story was going to end, but I didn't think it would be quite so tear-jerking! I simply *had* to give Bobby a boyfriend, if only to cheer myself up. ■

Life at a Glance

Author photograph by
Mark Pringle

BORN
Isle of Wight, 1962

EDUCATED
Winchester College; New College, Oxford

CAREER
After brief periods as a singing waiter, a typist and an encyclopedia ghostwriter, among other jobs, Gale published his first two novels, *Ease* and *The Aerodynamics of Pork*, simultaneously in 1986. He has since written eleven novels, including *Notes from an Exhibition*, *Rough Music* and *A Sweet Obscurity*; *Caesar's Wife*, a novella; and *Dangerous Pleasures*, a book of short stories.

LIVES
Cornwall

Top Eleven Books

1. *Persuasion*
   Jane Austen

2. *Middlemarch*
   George Eliot

3. *Tales of the City*
   Armistead Maupin

4. *The Bell*
   Iris Murdoch

5. *Collected Stories*
   Mavis Gallant

6. *The Wings of the Dove*
   Henry James

7. *Dinner at the Homesick Restaurant*
   Anne Tyler

8. *Remembrance of Things Past*
   Marcel Proust

9. *The Flint Anchor*
   Sylvia Townsend Warner

10. *The Woman in White*
    Wilkie Collins

11. *Collected Stories*
    Saki

A Walk around Winchester

by Patrick Gale

THIS IS THE first novel of mine set in Winchester, but anyone who knows my work and knows Winchester will have recognised a thinly veiled version of King Alfred's ancient capital in my previous novels, *Facing the Tank*, *Tree Surgery for Beginners* and *Friendly Fire*. Although I now live in deepest Cornwall, I'm a Hampshire Hog, born on the Isle of Wight and raised in Winchester. I left for university in 1980 but still think of Winchester as my home town. A short train ride from London Waterloo, Winchester makes for an excellent day out and the following route from the station will let you take in many of the locations drawn on in *The Whole Day Through* while enjoying the historic beauties of the city.

Emerging from the station, turn right, following the footpath along the top of the railway embankment and right again over the dizzyingly high railway bridge. Turn left at the other side and cross the road. You're now at the foot of Oram's Arbour, the site of an ancient encampment and where Ben takes the phone call from Chloë and, later, dawdles to watch children playing rounders. His and Bobby's house is down in Fulflood, across the Arbour to your right. Cross the grass on the diagonal path – you'll find a splendid view of the city spread out below you as you climb. Face away from the view and continue to the left at the top of the Arbour. Number 5 Clifton Road, the first of

the two houses with very steep gables, was
our first house in Winchester, where we lived
when I was a choirboy. Walk past the front
of the house and down Clifton Road to the
junction with Romsey Road. Up the hill to
your right lies the hospital where Ben works
– worth a detour if you're a fan of the
polychrome buildings of Butterworth – and
the prison where Hardy's Tess was hanged. ▶

*'Tatham's Gatehouse' by
Aidan Hicks – inspired by
Winchester College
Gatehouse. Copyright ©
Aidan Hicks 2005*

A Walk around Winchester (*continued*)

◀ If these don't tempt you, cross the road and continue along the pedestrianised delights of St James Terrace, where our lovers each walk in the book's final chapters. Across the railway cutting to your left is what was the Royal Green Jackets' barracks.

At the end of St James Terrace turn left down the hill and almost immediately on your right you'll see the corner house that was the model for Professor Jellicoe's naturist hideaway in the novel. As you can see I took tremendous liberties with the truth, but I hope you can see why the original house has always intrigued me. Carry on down St James Lane. You're now entering the area of the city dominated by my old school, Winchester College. You can see the magnificent bell tower rising out of the oldest part of the College straight ahead of you, but the school has grown so since its original foundation that many of the houses in this part of town are now part of it.

Cross Southgate Street, then continue directly down the hill by Canon Street. At the end of the street turn left then immediately right and continue along College Street, pausing, naturally, to browse in P. & G. Wells the Bookseller. A little way past Wells you'll find a pink house on your right where Jane Austen breathed her last. Her grave in the nearby cathedral mentions her Christian virtues and 'the extraordinary endowment of her mind' but avoids that tainted word *novelist*...

A minute's more walking brings you to the College's gatehouse and it's well worth taking one of the guided tours here. If you

Inspired by Winchester College's ringing chamber – by Aidan Hicks. Copyright © Aidan Hicks 2005

have an hour to spare, you can now visit the watermeadows and St Cross by carrying on along College Street, following the old red-brick wall that encloses the warden's garden. Where the wall turns sharply to the right you'll have a view to your left of elegant Wolvesey Palace, home of the bishop, and the vast ruins – now enclosing choir school playing fields – of the medieval palace it replaced. A part of the ruins is usually open to the public. Continue along the warden's wall, turning right and right again, to where the pavement brings you alongside the College's 1960s concert hall. The way into the College from this side is barred to you but you take a footpath to your left, alongside the river.

Winchester is a watery city and once had a network of brooks and streams usefully ▶

A Walk around Winchester (*continued*)

◄ cutting across it. Most of these have long since been channelled underground, leaving only street names to show where they run, but on this side of the city all the way out to the hospital at St Cross, water rules and you'll walk through scenery typical of Hampshire's south – water meadows rich in trout, herons and other wildlife. The footpath leads you alongside some of the College's playing fields.

St. Cross, Winchester
Project Gutenberg
copyright ©
www.gutenberg.net

The path crosses Garnier Road by the old pumping station and winds on, past moist gardens and allotments, to another stretch of water meadows beyond a kissing gate. Beyond you now lies St Cross Hospital. Well worth a visit for the partly Norman church (where Ben and Bobby attend Shirley's memorial service) and the lovely complex of old buildings surrounding it. You can spot the permanent residents by the red or black robes they're supposed to wear at all times. Traditionally any visitor can claim the Traveller's Dole – a chunk of bread and a glass of beer served free at the gate – but last time I checked this had been replaced by less frugal, non-charitable refreshments served in the outer courtyard.

At the end of your visit, walk almost straight ahead out of the outer gate, around a white fire barrier and on to Back Street. This will lead you past some delightful old houses, including a half-timbered one on a right-hand corner said to be one of the oldest in the city, past St Faith's Primary School (where I imagined Ben and Bobby's mother worked) and out on to Kingsgate Road. This seamlessly becomes Kingsgate Street, which you follow for its entire length. As the road progresses you'll see the cathedral's nave looming up ahead like a stone battleship. If you feel in need of sustenance, lunch can be found at the Queen's Head, which has a pleasant garden, or the extremely atmospheric and much older Wykeham Arms.

From the Wykeham Arms pass directly beneath the old gateway ahead of you. This houses St Swithun's, one of the city's tiniest but most atmospheric churches, reached by a steep flight of stairs. Turning right then brings you through the fifteenth-century Prior's Gate into the cathedral close and up against some of the oldest domestic buildings in it, including the Prior's Lodge. Just around the corner to the right lies Pilgrims' School, which educates the choristers for the cathedral and the quiristers for the College. To the left of the school's front door stands the Pilgrims' Hall, all that remains of the old medieval priory's guesthouse, well worth a peek if it's unlocked, for one of the earliest examples of a hammer-beam roof in the country.

Following the road on through the ▶

About the book

◄ close will bring you past the handsome deanery, much improved for one of Charles II's visits. Beyond that, keeping to the right, you will come to the Gothic arches that are all that remain of the eleventh-century chapter house. If it's a sunny day, slip through here to visit Dean Garnier's garden, which grants magnificent views of the cathedral exterior, as does the well-concealed path you can pick up by passing through the broad tunnel known as the Slype just beyond it.

Please don't follow Professor Jellicoe's disgraceful example by trying to slip in through the secure door in the Slype's middle – the code I give in the book is NOT the right one! Rather, retrace your steps and walk under the long line of flying buttresses along the cathedral nave and enter through the west end. This may be the tourists' entrance but it also confronts you with one of the most dramatic interior views the country can offer.

Leaving the cathedral by the way you came in, follow the lime avenue out of the close to The Square. Here you'll find one of the city's well-kept architectural secrets, the sister church to St Swithun's – St Lawrence-in-the-Square. Once a chapel royal for Norman kings, it's now principally a fifteenth-century building, crammed with earlier details, which charms for the Narnian fashion in which it seems to open out from a cupboard-like entrance between adjoining shops.

To return to the station, turn right as you come out of St Lawrence's, pause to admire the pinnacled splendour of the fifteenth-century Butter Cross, then head up the high street, past Elizabeth Frink's fetching horse and rider, as far as the Westgate, then cross the road beyond County Hall and its bronze hog and follow Station Road. The curious who still have the energy can visit the little Westgate Museum, then turn left to visit the splendid Great Hall and the long-since-disproved Arthurian Round Table... ■

Winchester Cathedral,
Winchester
Project Gutenberg
copyright ©
www.gutenberg.net

Spread the Light

'There are two ways of spreading light: to
be the candle or the mirror that reflects it.'

EDITH WHARTON

From Socrates to the salons of
pre-Revolutionary France, the great minds
of every age have debated the merits of
literary offerings alongside questions of
politics, social order and morality. Whether
you love a book or loathe it, one of the
pleasures of reading is the discussion books
regularly inspire. Below are a few suggestions
for topics of discussion about
The Whole Day Through . . .

✦ **Which character do you identify with in**
***The Whole Day Through*?**

✦ ***The Whole Day Through* is set during**
the course of a day with flashbacks to
past events. What are the effects of this
narrative technique?

✦ **Was Professor Jellicoe right to warn Ben**
off marriage? Do you think marriage or
domesticity can still get in the way of
ambition and career advancement?

✦ **Do you look after an elderly or disabled**
relative or do you need care yourself?
How does it make you feel? Is it the
responsibility of the family to look after
their loved ones or should society get
involved?

- ✦ Do you think there is prejudice against people with disabilities having a sex life? Why do you think this is?

- ✦ Can you blame Professor Jellicoe for Laura's failed relationships? What did you make of Laura's relationship with her father? To what extent do you blame your parents when things don't work out in your life?

- ✦ Was it nostalgia that made Laura and Ben fall in love again? Or desire? Would you have done the same in their position?

- ✦ How did you feel at the end of the book? Do you think Ben was right to stay with Chloë: is he a strong or a weak character? Is it a happy ending?

If You Loved This,
You Might Like . . .

Other titles by Patrick Gale

Notes from an Exhibition

Gifted artist Rachel Kelly is a whirlwind of
creative highs and anguished, crippling lows.
She's also something of an enigma to her
husband and four children. So when she is
found dead in her Penzance studio, leaving
behind some extraordinary new paintings,
there's a painful need for answers. Her
Quaker husband appeals for information on
the internet. The fragments of a shattered
life slowly come to light, and it becomes
clear that bohemian Rachel has left her
children not only a gift for art, but also her
haunting demons.

'Thought-provoking, sensitive, humane . . .
by the end I had laughed and cried and put
all his other books on my wish list'
Daily Telegraph

'Poised and pitch-perfect throughout, this
is an engrossing portrait of a troubled and
remarkable character. A fine writer at the
top of his game'
Mail on Sunday

Rough Music

As a small boy, Julian is taken on what
seems to be the perfect Cornish summer
holiday. It is only when he becomes a man –
seemingly at ease with love, with his sexuality, with his ghosts – that the traumatic
effects of that distant summer rise up to
challenge his defiant assertion that he is
happy and always has been.

....

'Hugely compelling. *Rough Music* is an
astute, sensitive and at times tragically
uncomfortable meditation on sex, lies
and family . . . a fabulously unnerving book'
Independent on Sunday

'More vivid and revealing than any snapshot,
faithfully illuminating the vicissitudes of the
heart, memory's fragility and the wear and
tear of habit on desire'   *Sunday Times*

Tree Surgery for Beginners

Lawrence Frost has neither father nor siblings, and fits so awkwardly into his worldly mother's life he might have dropped from the sky. Like many such heroes, he grows up happier with plants than people. Waking one morning to find himself branded a wife-beater and under suspicion of murder, his small world falls apart as he loses wife, daughter, liberty, livelihood and, almost, his mind. A darkly comic fairy tale for grown-ups.

'The book is one of [Gale's] best: a fluently constructed narrative underpinned by excellent characterisation. Running through it all is the theme of redemption; and the hero's journey from despair to hope makes a stirring odyssey for the reader'
Sunday Telegraph

'An adventurous but confidently handled book, which shows the wisdom of straying from the straight and narrow'   *The Times*

The Facts of Life

A young composer exiled from Germany
during World War II finds love and safety in
rural East Anglia only for tragedy to erupt
into his life. In prosperous and esteemed
old age, he must then watch as his wilful
grandchildren fall in love with the same
enigmatic and perhaps dangerous young
man – and learn life's harder lessons in
their turn.

'Gale is both a shameless romantic and hip
enough to get away with it. His moralised
narrative has as its counterpart a rigorous
underpinning of craft'   *New Statesman*

'It is impossible to put *The Facts of Life*
down. A rural English blockbuster. It is
beautifully done'   *Daily Telegraph*

A Sweet Obscurity

At nine years old, Dido has never known what it is like to be part of a proper family. Eliza, the clever but hopeless aunt who has brought her up, can't give her the normal childhood she craves. Eliza's ex, Giles, wants Dido back in his life, but his girlfriend has other ideas. Then an unexpected new love interest for Eliza causes all four to re-evaluate everything and sets in motion a chain of events which threatens to change all their lives.

....

'Gale's most questioning, ambitious work. It amuses and startles. *A Sweet Obscurity* is worth every minute of your time'
Independent

'Intriguing and impressive...A memorable study of a child forced cruelly, even tragically, to grow up too soon'   *Sunday Times*

The Cat Sanctuary

Torn apart by a traumatic childhood, sisters
Deborah and Judith are thrown back
together again when Deborah's diplomat
husband is accidentally assassinated. Judith's
lover Joanna, the instigator of this awkward
reunion, finds that as the sisters' murky past
is raked up, so too is her own, and the three
women become embroiled in a tangle of
passion and recrimination.

....

'*The Cat Sanctuary* is a book with claws. It
has a soft surface – a story set in sloping
Cornish countryside, touching on love,
families and forgiveness, delivered in a
gentle, straightforward prose – but from
time to time it catches you unawares. Scratch
the surface, suggests Gale, and you draw
blood'   *The Times*

'Engrossing ... Gale is a charmingly
idiosyncratic writer who could not write a
cliché if he tried'   *Daily Telegraph*

Find Out More

USEFUL WEBSITES

www.galewarning.org
Patrick Gale's own website in which you can
find out about his other books, read review
coverage, post your own reviews, leave
messages and contact other readers. There
are also diary listings to alert you to
Patrick's broadcasts or appearances and
a mailing list you can join.

www.nos.org.uk
The National Osteoporosis Society website.

www.downs-syndrome.org.uk
The Down's Syndrome Association website.

**www.visitwinchester.co.uk/site/tourist-
information**
All you need to retrace Ben and Laura's
steps.

What's next?

Tell us the name of an author you love

| Patrick Gale | Go ▶ |

and we'll find your next great book.

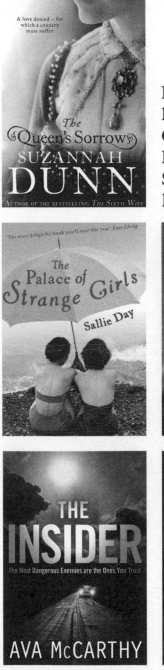

HAVE YOU READ THESE OTHER BOOKS FROM THE SAINSBURY'S BOOK CLUB?

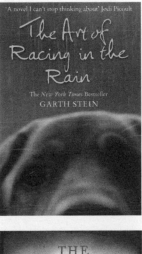